P9-CCK-014

The bomb truck lurched
on its suicide course

Vince Biondi was in the homestretch. He couldn't see the camp yet, but it wouldn't be long.

"I wonder if this will hurt," he said out loud.

The truck with the nuclear device roared down the straightaway at maximum speed. Biondi no longer steered the beast—he was just along for the ride.

The camp's gate came rushing at him.
Before he could blink, he was crashing into the compound, heading straight for the bunker ramp.

"God, I hope this is quick," Biondi said.

It was quick.

THE BUNKER

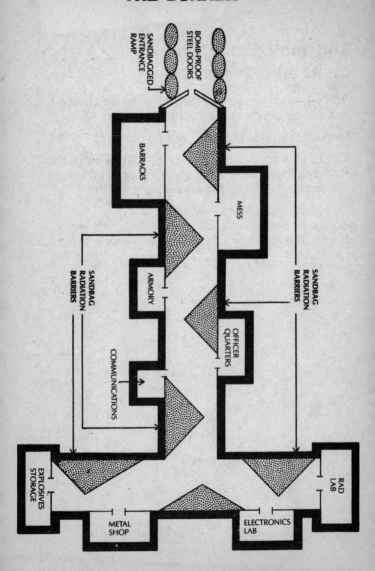

BOMB-PROOF STEEL DOORS

SANDBAGGED ENTRANCE RAMP

BARRACKS

MESS

SANDBAG RADIATION BARRIERS

ARMORY

OFFICER QUARTERS

SANDBAG RADIATION BARRIERS

COMMUNICATIONS

EXPLOSIVES STORAGE

METAL SHOP

ELECTRONICS LAB

RAD LAB

SOBs

THE
PLAINS OF FIRE

JACK HILD

A GOLD EAGLE BOOK FROM
W RLDWIDE

TORONTO · NEW YORK · LONDON · PARIS
AMSTERDAM · STOCKHOLM · HAMBURG
ATHENS · MILAN · TOKYO · SYDNEY

First edition February 1984

ISBN 0-373-61602-3

Special thanks and acknowledgment to Alan Philipson
for his contributions to this work.

1

Dr. Hussein al-Barani was being dragged screaming across the camp compound. His broken legs trailed limply behind him, his bloody bare feet scraping faint furrows in the desert gravel. As the pair of Islamic Revolutionary Guards hauled him along, they mocked the shrill noises he made. The slightly built, fifty-three-year-old astrophysicist could not choke down his cries, not even to deny his tormentors their pleasure. The pain that flashed up with the sudden shifting of shattered bones obliterated his will.

He was thrown belly down before the camp's military overseer, Captain Mohamadi Razod of the Pasdaran. At once the sole of Razod's boot came down on the back of Dr. al-Barani's head. His nose and mouth flattened against the sun-blasted stones. His shrieks were instantly smothered. For a full minute he was conscious only of the relentless downward pressure on his skull, the rock fragments gouging into his face and the desperation burning in his lungs. Then the angle of force changed. His head was wrenched to one side, allowing him to gasp for breath.

"Look at the chair," Razod said.

Dr. al-Barani blinked tears from his eyes, squinted against the glare, the shimmering waves of heat. The chair was made of wood and had no arms. It was perched atop a crude pyramid of heaped scrap lumber. Around it were dozens more Pasdars in gray-brown camouflage uniforms. One of them stood with his boot propped on a red jerrican of gasoline.

"If you confess now," Razod said, "you will avoid a terrible unpleasantness."

Dr. al-Barani shivered. Though the afternoon sun flailed the desolate Iranian plain, he felt a powerful chill. With every fiber of his body he wanted to live, yet he knew death was the only rational choice for him. He closed his eyes and moistened his dusty lips. Then he spoke words he had repeated countless times during the past week. Words that beatings and torture had not altered.

"I have nothing to confess."

The boot was removed from his head.

Razod gestured abruptly at the Pasdars. Strong hands lifted Dr. al-Barani by the armpits. Again he was dragged and cries he could not contain burst from his throat as his shattered legs trailed over rougher ground. He was hoisted up and dropped on the seat of the chair. His arms were twisted around the chair back and pinned behind it.

In quiet defiance, he slowly raised his head.

From his elevated position, Dr. al-Barani could take in the entire camp; he saw it with the perfect clarity of the doomed. The camp perimeter was defined by three twenty-foot-high fences, concentric rings of electrified razor wire spaced ten feet apart. The guard towers and the domes of the prefab outbuildings were painted in a camouflage pattern. The gateway to the bunker complex was a hundred yards away, at the extreme rear of the compound, nestled at the foot of a wide saddle between a pair of low mountains. In the shimmering heat, all colors and shapes in the landscape seemed to be the work of nature. Then, from the sandbagged entrance, a group of men in white lab coats emerged, moving briskly toward him. Leading the way was Dr. Hamid, al-Barani's oldest friend.

His betrayer.

"They have asked permission to watch," Razod explained.

Dr. al-Barani stared at the captain, at the false smile that peeled his lips back from his white teeth. Razod dearly loved his work, loved to slowly twist the bowel-buried knife. He was almost as much taken with himself. From a distance his dark good looks were striking; up close that first impression was erased by the moonlike cratering that covered his cheeks, and the dead cold of his black eyes. He had risen from the ranks of the Hizballah, the followers of the Party of God, a mob of unwashed urban poor who, after the revolution, prowled Tehran's streets searching for dissidents, unbelievers, to club to death. Razod was not intelligent, but he was clever. He had learned how to make men afraid. In postrevolutionary Iran his future was assured.

"Make way for the scientists," Razod said, motioning for the milling Pasdars to stand aside.

Dr. Hamid trudged doggedly forward, walking the gauntlet of off-duty guardsmen. His lab coat was open, the buttons of his white dress shirt stretched to the bursting point across his pot belly. Under bushy, graying eyebrows his expression was determined, grim.

Dr. al-Barani tried to meet his old friend's gaze. It was impossible. Hamid was looking through him, eyes focused on the great evil he represented. The astrophysicist felt a surge of anger. Not at Hamid for bowing to the inevitable, but at himself for not anticipating it. In all their years together at university in Paris, in all the time they had spent laying the groundwork for the Shah's nuclear-power program, he had never really understood Hamid. The man's obvious flaws he had forgiven. The brilliant often had their quirks of character, allowing themselves to be blinded by good intentions, by their commitment to science and reason.

Dr. al-Barani was a man of great intelligence, but he was not clever. In postrevolutionary Iran he had no future at all.

"If you scholars are ready," Razod said to Hamid.

The mathematician gave a curt nod. Behind him, the other scientists stood shoulder to shoulder, a knot of white in a field of camouflage fatigues.

"Strip him," the captain ordered.

Hands ripped at the doctor's waist. He howled and writhed as his trousers were jerked down over his broken legs. His bare limbs were swollen, covered by massive purple bruises, marks left by boot heels that had stomped over and over again until his bones had finally snapped. Naked from the waist down, the astrophysicist faced his inquisitor and the massed spectators.

Mohamadi Razod beamed at him. "You have been accused of doing the work of Amrika, the Great Satan," he said, "of attempting to undermine the revolutionary spirit of your co-workers. If you give me the truth, tell me who helped you, who paid you, I may be persuaded to overlook your crimes."

Dr. al-Barani shook his head. He knew Razod would overlook nothing. If he confessed, the punishment would not end on the pyre. There would be more victims. Innocent victims. His wife. His teenage daughter and infant son. The Government of God would routinely hand them all over to men like Razod. The idea was unthinkable. His family's only hope for survival was his silence. The only way he could guarantee that silence was to die.

"In my whole life," he said, "I have committed one crime. Allah forgive me, it was my contribution to this project."

"Nail him down!" Razod snarled.

One of the Pasdars produced a hammer and a four-inch spike. Dr. al-Barani moaned as two other soldiers wedged his thighs apart. The man with the hammer roughly positioned Dr. al-Barani's genitals on the seat, setting the point of the nail high on his scrotum, between his testicles, then swung the hammer down. With a single blow he drove the nail point through thin layers of skin, into and through the chair seat.

"Release his arms," Razod said.

Dr. al-Barani stared down at the round head and inch of nail sticking up between his legs. He was pinned like a butterfly neatly and carefully, permanently intact. The pain was nothing compared to what he had already been through. Pushed to the limit, his mind gave him distance from his agony. He was in shock.

He was brought around by the unmistakable odor of gasoline. A Pasdar was sloshing the contents of the jerrican over the left side of the pyramid. As the man poured, the assembled guardsmen began clapping their hands and chanting.

"Death! Death! Death!"

Not to be outshone in zeal, the scientists also took up the cheer, shouting at the top of their lungs, stamping their feet.

Dr. al-Barani fought down waves of nausea. Death was what he wanted; it was also what he knew he deserved. His equations were the key to the entire project. Without them, the chemical and electrical engineers, the mathematicians, the metallurgists, the high-explosive technologists could never have succeeded. Thanks to him, the most terrible weapon in the history of mankind was now in the hands of brutal, ignorant fanatics.

Razod took a box of wooden matches from his fatigue pants. He presented it to Hamid. "The honor is yours, professor. You have earned it."

The color drained from Hamid's face.

The captain smiled. "Unless, of course, you still feel some sympathy for this traitor to Islam."

Sympathy was unthinkable.

Sympathy was suicide.

Hamid accepted the matches. His fingers trembled so violently that the match he struggled to light went out at once.

Dr. al-Barani watched his comrade fumble with a second match. Hamid kept his eyes downcast, unable to face the man he was about to execute. How different Hamid had seemed on the eve of revolution, standing up boldly for ideas, principles, but standing in a crowd. Everyone was on the same side, then. The intellectuals, the shopkeepers, the young, the homeless, all banded together against the Shah and SAVAK, his hated secret police. In 1979, Dr. al-Barani had had high hopes for constructive change in his country, for a moral rebirth of its people. He had accepted the repression of the new regime, had willingly agreed to work in isolation at the remote camp because he believed that the threat from hostile neighbors and the superpowers was real. He had agreed because he had believed that the nuclear devices would only be used as a last line of defense.

His naiveté was criminal.

As work on the devices neared completion, secrecy relaxed and Dr. al-Barani discovered that the weapons were going to be used offensively, in a first strike against civilian targets. Horrified, he went straight to Hamid and tried to convince him to shut down the project immediately, that the two of them, as senior members of the research team, could and must organize the other scientists to stop work.

Hamid would not listen to him.

He could not make the mathematician see the monstrous evil they were both part of. He could not make him understand that the scientists involved in the project were living on borrowed time. The regime had no intention of mass-producing atomic bombs. There were only enough raw materials and components for four of them and once those four were finished, so were the scientists. Contaminated by Western thought and values they were a necessary evil; when they were no longer necessary they would be destroyed.

Ironically, science again intervened for Hamid. He did not have to touch the lighted match to the gasoline-soaked wood. As he brought it close, the pungent vapor ignited and half the pyre exploded in orange flame. In his conscience Hamid had faltered. Chemistry had murdered his friend.

A wall of withering heat slammed into Dr. al-Barani. Instinctively, he cringed as far away from the blaze and the oily black smoke as the nail would allow.

Razod stepped quickly to the unlit side of the piled wood, pulled his survival knife from its belt sheath and slapped it handle-first into the astrophysicist's right palm.

"Go ahead," the captain said. "Free yourself."

The Pasdars roared their approval.

Dr. al-Barani stared at the knife in his hand. The choice being offered was clear: to survive the flames he had to leave his testicles behind.

Over the hiss and snap of the fire he could hear the guardsmen shouting at him and laughing. They were sure that a weakling, an intellectual, would choose life at any price, even self-mutilation. As for Mohamadi Razod, he was counting on it. The captain wanted nothing more than to prolong his captive's agony, to ruin and disfigure him inch by inch.

Dr. al-Barani had realized early on in the interrogation that there was no further information the Pasdaran was seeking to corroborate. The only testimony against him was Hamid's. The torture had no point except as an outlet for Razod's hatred of the educated.

The joke was on Razod.

When Hamid had refused to help put an end to the project, Dr. al-Barani had sought aid elsewhere. On his last visit home he had met with an American intelligence operative in Tehran. He had given the man details of the project and its barbaric aims. In return he had received a promise that what he had done would be undone. That the bombproof bunker in the sea of stones and all the twisted creatures that inhabited it would be wiped off the face of the earth.

Beneath the doctor's feet the fire was spreading, rapidly eating its way through the heap of lumber. The hairs on the outside of his left arm and leg turned to ash as the wind swept flame across them. The heat was unbearable. He could wait no longer.

Dr. al-Barani raised the knife. Razod's eyes searched the doctor's face greedily, looking for signs of terror and panic.

There were none.

Dr. al-Barani set the blade's razor edge to the

side of his throat and slashed in a precise arc. From ear to ear his flesh sprang open in a gaping wound. Hot blood gushed from the severed jugular and carotid, splashing down his chest and arms.

Razod let out a howl of rage.

It was the last sound Dr. al-Barani heard. Blackness enveloped him, erasing the pain, lifting him away.

By the time Razod commandeered a guardsman's Heckler and Koch assault rifle, what sat in the smoking chair was no longer a man. The captain's victim had escaped in front of half the camp.

Beside himself with fury, Razod cocked the weapon and fired anyway, emptying the entire 30-round magazine, blowing the corpse apart.

There were no cheers when the gunshot echoes faded. Only the crackle of the bonfire, the whistle of the hot wind. Razod hurled the assault rifle to the ground.

Though he did not know it yet, more than face was lost.

All was lost.

2

"You're eight minutes late," the pretty blonde said as she pushed back her typing chair. "The senator doesn't like to be kept waiting."

Walker Jessup gave the secretary a broad smile. And no apology. He had spent the last quarter hour in the building's underground parking garage, sitting in his BMW Bavaria, rewinding stereo cassette tapes so he could arrive precisely when he had. As far as he was concerned, the senator could stick punctuality squarely up his ass.

Jessup tried to maintain eye contact when the blonde stood up, but the lure of the scenery twelve inches down was too much for him. The young lady did not appreciate his interest in her chest. She did an abrupt about-face and headed for the massive mahogany door.

Body language, he thought. Under the sleek, gray knit dress the tight swing of the secretary's hips spoke volumes.

All on the same theme.

No way, Jessup.

She opened the door for him and stepped aside.

The senator was facing the suite's tall windows, his hands locked behind his back, rocking up and down on heels that secretly adjusted his height from five foot five to five foot eight. Even so, he had to look up to met the big Texan's gaze.

Way up.

As the door clicked shut behind Jessup, the senator said, "Sit." He indicated the armchair across from his wide desk. "We have a problem."

Jessup eased his considerable bulk into the red leather upholstered chair. A normal-sized person might have found the chair comfortable. For Jessup, the fit was tight enough to impede his breathing. "What sort of problem?"

The senator stepped to his desk and tapped a manila file folder lying on the blotter. For Your Eyes Only was stamped across the front of the file. "The committee has just received some alarming information from Iran. . . ."

Jessup fought the grin that threatened to spread over his face. "You mean that they've got the bomb?"

The senator scowled at him and Jessup watched the vein just under the skin of the senator's right temple grow fat, a squiggly blue worm. He did not bother to question how Jessup had got hold of news that was supposed to have a Top Secret Crypto classification. The Texan had worked with both military and civilian Intelligence before going into business for himself. He maintained an elaborate network of personal contacts in the international fraternity of spies, mercenaries and criminal low life. On the Hill he was known as "The Fixer," a guy who could arrange anything, anywhere—for the right price. The senator righteously despised both the man and his methods. And he hated the idea that the United States had to resort to using men like Jessup to get critical, dirty jobs done. But most of all, he hated Jessup's perfect record of success.

"We have verified through both black and white sources," the senator continued, "that our information is reliable. The committee's analysts are only just beginning to figure out how Iran managed it."

"That's not too hard to guess."

"Really? Then you explain it to me. I'd like to know how a country fresh from a revolution and involved in an exhausting border war could come up with the wherewithal to embark on, let alone complete, a nuclear-weapons program." The senator made a move to sit down in his high-backed executive swivel chair but thought better of it. With Jessup seated and himself standing, he did not have to look up at the man.

"I suggest you go over your white sources again, senator," Jessup said. He was referring to the body of unclassified material in technical and general-interest publications, sources available to any and all comers, that typically made up eighty percent of all intelligence gathering. "It takes raw material and technology to make a nuclear bomb. The Shah left a lot of both. He was real big on nuclear-power plants, if you remember. Planned to have twenty in operation by 1990. As I recall, you were real big on handing him the stuff to build them with."

"The world situation was quite different, then," the senator replied testily. "It was a matter of supplying our know-how to a valued ally or letting other countries do it." He puffed out his narrow chest. "I have a lifelong record of commitment to American industry and American workers. There was no way of predicting this outcome."

Jessup didn't hide his boredom. There was no way of publicly predicting the outcome in Iran and keeping a seat in the legislature. Better to prop up the shaky regime, look strong and "committed" to the home folks and get reelected.

First things came first.

"Men who can put together a nuclear reactor," Jessup went on, "can build an atomic bomb. Most of the necessary components were probably already there."

"Components? What are you talking about? They didn't get those from us."

"They didn't have to. Check your white sources. The Shah was South Africa's main supplier of oil. South Africa has been producing weapons-grade plutonium and uranium from its Valindaba plant for years. For all anyone knows, the Shah got one of the first shipments. Both he and South Africa had a strong interest in maintaining Iran's status quo.''

The senator took a pair of bifocals from the vest of his gray pin-striped suit and put them on. He could feel control of the meeting slipping away, and he was determined not to let that happen. He flipped open the file folder and scanned the tissue-thin pages. ''According to the committee's information, there are four operational weapons. They intend to move the bombs to populated targets and detonate them. Their level of technology is very crude, roughly what we had at Hiroshima-Nagasaki. Each of the weapons has to weigh several tons. External dimensions could be as much as five by ten feet. They have no reliable airborne delivery system for a payload of that size. No missile they've got could carry one.''

''And a manned aircraft,'' Jessup added, ''would have to penetrate ground-to-air and air-to-air defenses.''

The senator closed the file. ''We estimate these weapons to be in the 20- to 40-kiloton range. Perhaps twice as powerful as Fat Man, the Nagasaki bomb. One of them is powerful enough to kill tens of thousands. Maybe more, depending on where and when it's exploded.''

''One could be enough to start a jihad,'' the

Texan said, "a holy war that could suck in the whole Middle East."

"Or, failing that," the senator countered, "the remaining bombs could be used to blackmail the West into submission."

"Sounds like a job for Delta Team."

"No, that's completely out of the question. We can't use an official U.S. military unit."

Jessup knew that. If the committee could have dumped this one into the lap of the Rapid Deployment Force, he would not be sitting where he was now.

"This mission demands an incursion into the sovereign territory of Iran."

"An act of war."

"Let's say it would seriously jeopardize other sensitive negotiations in the area."

"You mean scuttle," Jessup said. Scuttle was also what it would do to the senator's carefully cultivated, peace-at-any-price public image.

"The committee wants your private covert-action team to handle this. The job has to be completed in the next fourteen days, before any of the weapons can be moved from the research site. Are they available?"

Jessup held the senator in his sleepy gaze.

It was crow-eating time.

"I take it the committee had no complaints about the outcome of the SOBs' first mission in Kaluba?"

The senator was at a sudden, rare loss for

words. It burned him no end that Jessup's small, handpicked band of mercenaries had succeeded in restoring democracy to the south African country. He had given them an almost impossible task in the hope that they would fail, be killed or captured, thereby reinforcing his well-known position on the futility of violent covert action. Diplomacy, not confrontation—that was the campaign rhetoric that had returned him to office four times. It sounded like a moral stand. It was not. The senator was all for diplomacy only because that happened to be his little corner of Washington. Diplomacy got him headlines. Headlines got him more power.

"We were satisfied," he said tightly. "This Iranian mission, I think you'll agree, is much more difficult. It calls for an undetected deep penetration into forbidden territory, the capture and destruction of all nuclear weapons, research equipment and associated personnel. And it has to look like an accident."

"A what?"

The senator's thin lips twisted into a smile. "On this the committee is in unanimous agreement. We want it to look like a nuclear accident. An inadvertent detonation of one of the devices. That way we will not only eliminate Iran's hopes of every pursuing this idea further, but we will put the fear of God into other would-be nuclear nations. Give them an object lesson that things can go wrong when you play with atomic fire. Disastrously wrong."

Jessup nodded. "I like it."

"And speaking of things going wrong, I don't think I need to warn you that this country could not stand another hostage-rescue-type fiasco. Officially sanctioned or not."

At one point in his life, Walker Jessup would have punched the senator's face to pulp for such a remark. After all, it was coming from the mouth of one of the Capitol Hill doves who had voted down funds to train and arm a Delta Team force prior to the hostage taking. The senator had been a leader in the opposition to such a unit. As much as any man alive, he was to blame for the tragic loss of eight brave men. But Walker Jessup was no longer a hot blood. He did not have the body for it anymore. His life-style and his love for thoughtfully prepared food had started to catch up with him about the time he got out of Vietnam. He was still an incredibly powerful man, but his hand speed was gone. Hand speed did not mean squat on the Hill, anyway. Head speed was what counted.

And Jessup was no man to mess with in that department.

Instead of caving in the senator's bridgework, the big Texan unleashed a much more devastating blow.

A gut shot.

"This is going to cost you people an arm and a leg," he said.

The senator's face turned white, then flushed

with anger. He snatched the bifocals off his nose and stabbed them at Jessup. "The price per mission has already been agreed upon. Fifty thousand dollars per man plus expenses. I think that is exceptionally generous considering these men aren't much more than criminals with military training."

"They're a lot more than that, but that's beside the point," Jessup said evenly, pushing out of the chair and standing up. He looked down at the little man in the thousand-dollar suit. "The price has not been agreed upon. Each job is different. If you want this one done, you're going to have to give me an open checkbook to work from."

"Unlimited finances?"

Jessup loved to hear this man whine.

"I wouldn't even consider offering the job to Barrabas without it."

The senator paced back and forth behind his desk for a moment, walking between the flags of his home state and the nation, past framed mementos of more than two decades of power-brokering in the strongest country on earth. He was looking for an angle, a lever with which to gain advantage. This covert mission was infinitely more suicidal than the first. There was every chance that all hands would be lost with accompanying adverse publicity. Everything could fall the senator's way. The only real problem was the cash outlay. Then he had it.

"All right, all right," the senator said, waving his hands in apparent surrender. "Have it your way. But keep a lid on the expenses somehow. The pressure on us to trim our operating budgets is incredible."

Jessup said nothing. He knew how the senator would interpret austerity. The red-white-and-blue flag the senator was standing in front of would go before the stuck-up blonde with the D cups.

"And no matter what the bottom-line figure is," the senator went on, "offer them one-third up front and keep the rest in reserve for payment on completion of the mission."

"I'll do my best," Jessup lied.

As far as he was concerned, if Nile Barrabas wanted a piece of this, he could write his own goddamn ticket.

3

Erika Dykstra returned to the side of the rumpled bed. In her right hand she held the early edition of the *International Herald-Tribune*. The paper was folded open to the classified personal ads. Soft, fog-filtered morning light swept across the naked man sleeping on his back. It accentuated the deep indentations, the "cuts" of muscle, tendon, sinew. Though it was a magnificent body, it was no longer perfect. The places Nile Barrabas had been, the things he had done had left their marks on him. Erika had never counted the scars, but she knew each one. By touch.

His thick hair was almost completely white, a striking contrast to the deep tan of his skin. They had been friends, lovers, since the last months in Vietnam and she had never seen his hair any other color. That, too, was a scar of sorts, the result of a head wound.

At the time, Saigon gossip claimed that the shock of the injury had done something to his mind as well, made him "boo coo dinky dau." Very, very crazy. After he had recovered and returned to combat, he had done wild, dangerous things, had courted death with savagery and lust. It was a madness she had learned to respect.

Erika Dykstra was twenty-seven years old, a Dutch national, an Amsterdam native. Like her brother, Gunther, she was an accomplished international smuggler, specializing in gold, gems, works of art and, occasionally, armament. She had seen and done things that most people never even dreamed about. And she had learned.

There were turning points in life.

A lucky card.

A face in the crowd.

A close brush with death.

She also knew that some wounds never healed.

As Barrabas slept, his eyes shifted under heavy lids. He was determined, even in sleep. The stark planes of his face caught and held the light. Cheekbones, chin, brow were chiseled, jutting. Immovable.

Erika looked at the empty liter bottle of Jenever on the bed table beside him. They had started on the Dutch gin together. He had finished it after she had fallen asleep. Barrabas drank a lot, by anyone's standards. Over the past week he had been outdoing himself. She never said a word about it; Erika was a realist. She knew she could not mother a man like Nile Barrabas. She could not hold or keep him, either. Though, at times, a tiny hopelessly irrational part of her wanted to do just that. When she was with him it was all out, one hundred percent. She could not ask for more than that.

The weeks since his last mission had been one long party. They had spent a lot of time and money in Paris, raiding the shops along the Champs-Elysées, motor-sailing on the Seine, eating elaborate late-night dinners in the city's finest bistros. But the most fun of all were the seven days they had on the Isle of Capri. They stayed at a hotel that dangled precariously from the island's mountain peak. They had done some tourist things, hiked, swam, but mostly made slow, gentle love in their room overlooking the ruins of Tiberius's estate, lush green vineyards and the aquamarine sea.

She loved him more than any man she had ever known. But he was not for her. Nile Barrabas needed things even she could not understand. Maybe he *was* crazy. Addicted like some junkie to the risks of his profession.

Christ, she thought, what did that make her, then?

She glanced at the newspaper, at the personal ad she had circled in pencil. It was the ad Barrabas had been waiting for. The call to a new mission. She reached out to touch him, to wake him up, but drew her hand back. The ad was the end for them. Once she showed it to him, their private interlude would be over. He would still be in her bed, in her Amsterdam house, but she would have lost him. Until next time.

If there was a next time.

Erika dropped the paper to the floor. She untied the sash of her short blue silk robe and let the garment slip from her shoulders. The cool morning air made her nipples draw up into hard, sensitive points. Her body ached for him.

Afterward, she told herself as she pushed the tangled sheets aside. She would tell him afterward.

NILE BARRABAS STEPPED UP on the curb, out of the path of the blue-and-white police minivan. The pair of helmeted officers inside hardly gave him a glance as they passed. In a khaki nylon jacket and loose-fitting blue jeans, he was anybody and nobody. The minivan's taillights disappeared some sixty feet away as the narrow cobblestone street wound sharply to the right. Amsterdam cops did not hassle people without a reason. Even at night in Walletjes, the Centrum's red-light district.

Barrabas continued along the sidewalk, cutting around and between the parked cars. The one-way street was just wide enough for a single car. All parking had to be done over the curb. The architects of Warmoesstraat could be forgiven the oversight. Four hundred years ago there was no way of foreseeing the need for parking. The grimy, soot-blackened five-story buildings that lined the street were jammed together, wall against wall. The solid row of steeply sloping roofs looked like the teeth of a gigantic saw.

Ahead, pink flashing lights circled the sign of a small porno shop sandwiched between a pair of warehouses. The shop window was a clutter of dildoes and inflatable girlfriends. Barrabas hardly gave it a glance. He was on edge, wound up tight.

A soldier without a war.

The tension had crept up on him slowly. The way it always did, sooner or later. He could only take so much R and R before he started feeling useless, out of his element, before the party and the booze turned into escape and evasion.

Nile Barrabas did not kid himself about much of anything. He knew he could not function as a normal human being anymore. He had too many battles under his belt for that. Outside the world's free fire zones everything seemed so thin, so two-dimensional to him, almost like he could put his fist right through it.

Three doors down, the window display was much more interesting. The ground-floor apartment was occupied by a long-legged, red-haired prostitute. The drapes to her tiny front room were drawn back, and she sat on a high stool. She was dressed in a black lace bra and matching miniskirt. As Barrabas looked in, the young woman flashed him a wicked grin and let her thighs slip apart. Under the miniskirt her pubic mound was shaved as clean and smooth as a baby's behind.

Barrabas did a double take, then laughed out loud. For a moment at least, the tension that gripped him was gone. "Thanks, I needed that," he said to her.

The redhead could not understand him through the glass. She gestured for him to come inside. He shook his head and blew her a farewell kiss. She opened her legs wider as if to catch it.

There was no denying the Dutch were a friendly people.

As he moved deeper into the red-light district, he was offered other delights by the growing number of pedestrians. Sex of all varieties. Drugs. Stolen property. He continued down Warmoesstraat in the direction of the train station until he came to a row of shabby student hotels. The one he entered was called the Parima.

The lower floor was taken up by a seedy restaurant-bar. The decor was rotting fishnets and corks, the lighting blood red. Heavy-metal rock music blared from the jukebox. The Parima's clientele was made up of international student-dopers, pushers and whores in full war-paint.

Barrabas recognized Walker Jessup from behind. The man was built like a mountain.

A mountain of flab.

Barrabas slipped into the booth, sitting down opposite the former CIA man.

Jessup gave him a pained look. "Of all the places in Amsterdam to pick for a meeting," he

said. He pointed at the plate of untouched food
before him, then at the black bartender playing
with a baby chimpanzee on the bar. "I found a
pile of goddamn monkey fur in my herring."

"So, send it back."

Jessup scowled. "In a shithole like this, if you
complain about the food, it comes back with
monkey piss on it."

"Added flavor without added calories. Could
be an improvement."

The big Texan discreetly covered the fish with
his paper napkin. "Is it safe to drink the liquor
here?"

"As long as we crack the seal on the bottle
ourselves," Barrabas said.

"Is it still Scotch?"

"Mother's milk."

Jessup called for a full bottle of Johnnie
Walker Red Label. The bartender brought the
whiskey and two glasses. The chimp carried the
bill. Jessup grimaced when he read it, whipped
out a wad of multicolored bills and scattered a
few large-denomination notes in the bartender's
direction.

After the man left he said, "Now I know why
you wanted to come here. For every sucker you
steer in you get a cut on the liquor markup,
right?"

Barrabas checked the bottle's seal, then broke
it and filled the glasses to the top. Jessup knew
damn well why he had picked the Parima. It was

a place where everybody was either too stoned, too horny or too stupid to give a shit about anything. A dump site for the toxic waste of the "me" generation.

Before Jessup could get his glass to his lips Barrabas had tossed down four ounces of aged Scotch. The Texan knocked back his drink in two quick gulps. "This isn't going to be a contest, is it?" he said, beaming.

"No. No contest." Barrabas turned his empty glass upside down on the table. Fun and games time was over.

"Suit yourself, but I'm sure as hell not going to pass up seventy-five-dollar-a-bottle Scotch," Jessup said, refilling his own glass.

"Let's hear what you've got for me," Barrabas said.

Jessup sipped at his whiskey, then leaned forward, putting his elbows on the table. "It's a real cute one. The boys on the Hill want the SOBs to scratch a certain Third World nation's nuclear-arms program."

"What nation?"

"Iran."

Jessup carefully watched the ex-colonel's eyes as he spoke the one-word answer. For a split second he thought he saw a reaction, but it was gone so fast he could not be sure. There was no other response from Barrabas as Jessup described the suicidal parameters of the mission. The former CIA man would have been surprised if there had been.

The man sitting across the table from him was more than a professional soldier for hire. He was the kind of charismatic figure who could lead others, much less skilled than himself, grinning into the bowels of hell. The confidence he inspired was not just a matter of his training, his appearance, his track record. Nile Barrabas was always a mental step or two ahead. In combat he moved with a certainty that was uncanny.

Barrabas interrupted Jessup's recitation only once.

"How much time do we have?" he asked.

"A couple of weeks, on the outside. This job has to be completed ASAP, before any part of the nuclear arsenal can be moved away from the research site. We want containment and total destruction. And I repeat, the detonation has to look like an accident. That means you're in and out without a trace."

"And no survivors."

"No survivors."

Barrabas reached inside his jacket and took out a flat cigar case. He opened it and offered Jessup a hand-rolled panatella.

After they had both lit up, he said, "It's time to talk money."

"I'm listening."

Barrabas puffed at his cigar. "I want $200,000 per man."

Even though Jessup had been expecting a large figure, he was momentarily stunned. And showed it. "Shit, that's more than a couple of million."

"Head of class, Jessup."

"I was instructed to pay you one-third up front and the rest on successful completion of the mission."

Barrabas gave him a doubtful look. "Sounds like the boys on the Hill don't think much of our chances."

"Do you?"

Barrabas ignored the question.

"It's got to be sixty-forty," he said. "With a quarter of a million for expenses. I'll need access to the expense account by tomorrow afternoon."

"That's your last word?"

Barrabas leaned back and laced his fingers behind his head. He shifted his cigar to the corner of his mouth, then clenched his teeth so it stuck almost straight up in the air. "Yep, take it or stuff it."

A wide grin spread over Jessup's meaty face. He was thinking about the senator. He'd need his rubber jockey shorts when he got the bill for this escapade.

"The government accepts," he said.

Barrabas turned over his glass. "I'll drink to that."

Jessup filled the tumbler with Scotch and topped off his own. He made damn sure he got it all down in one swallow, too.

No sooner had the glass hit the tabletop than

Barrabas was pouring again. "I've got plenty of room for you on this mission, Jessup," he said. "How about it, want to tag along? Keep your hand in?"

Jessup chewed his cigar as if actually considering the offer. "Fuck you," he said.

Barrabas laughed.

The soldier had himself a war.

4

Liam O'Toole's heart was trying to drive his Adam's apple up into his mouth as he knocked on the chipped and scarred green door. The Belfast neighborhood that surrounded him was much grittier, meaner than he remembered; the row houses smaller, like brick rabbit hutches. The three houses directly across the street were gutted, sheet plywood nailed up over smoke-blackened window and door openings. At the curb a burned-out car sat on its brake drums.

The old neighborhood was a combat zone.

The green door slipped back a crack. A tiny, white-haired lady in a plastic flower-print apron stared up at him through thick spectacles. "I don't need any," she said.

"Mum, it's me, Liam."

She opened the door a bit wider and examined his face.

And O'Toole hers. He was shocked to see what twenty years had done, the wrinkles, the splotches. And he was glad he had decided to come back. To make his peace with her before it was too late.

"It's your son, Liam," he said. "Don't you remember me?"

The magnification of the heavy glasses made her eyes look huge. "I've no son by that name."

"Oh, for Christ's sake," O'Toole said. "You know who I am."

"Aye, I know who you are," she told him. "You're a damned murderer and no son of mine."

She slammed the door in his face.

"Please," he said. He could hear the door being bolted and chained on the other side. "Please listen to me. I've brought money to get you out of here. To buy you a little cottage in County Cork. Mum, let me in. We've got to talk."

Her thin voice answered through the door. "I want none of your blood money. I want none of you, either. Not for as long as I live."

"Mum? Mum?"

There was no reply. Only the sound of shuffling footsteps receding deeper into the house. He looked through the window beside the door, through yellowed lace curtains. It was exactly as he remembered it, the furniture, the photographs on the narrow fireplace mantel, the odd bits of ceramic bric-a-brac. His mother had always kept everything in its place.

His was on the outside, looking in.

The broad-shouldered, red-haired man looked silently at the bolted door and the history it denied him. Life for him would only be a series of todays and on this one he needed a drink. A lot of drinks.

The corner pub was ancient, with dark wood beams supporting the low ceiling, the air heavy with tobacco smoke and liquor fumes. The small, round wooden tables were occupied by serious boozers, most of them solitary, brooding over pints of Guinness. He stepped up to the bar.

"Give me a double Bushmill's neat with water back," he told the bartender.

The Irish whiskey he did in with a quick flip of the wrist. He took a tiny sip of water, winced, then asked for another double.

Liam O'Toole was a certified demolitions expert.

He was also something of a poet and philosopher. As such, he recognized the bitter irony of his professional calling.

One of the many things he had expertly demolished was his own life. Everything he touched, other than explosives, invariably turned to shit, a combination of bad temper and bad timing.

He had convinced himself that somehow over the span of two decades the gulf between his mother and himself had miraculously closed. That she would finally forgive him his stint with the IRA. He should have known better. The two of them were cut from the same cloth.

Hardheads.

If the police had not picked him up when he was seventeen as a suspected terrorist, taken him to a station back room and kicked the holy crap out of him, he would never have seriously considered taking up with the IRA. As it was, that was the first thing the innocent young man did when he was released.

You did not beat up Liam O'Toole for nothing.

The IRA taught him soldiering and gave him the basics of bomb making. He found he had a knack for it. But when he saw how his deadly toys were being used, he quit the organization. Killing members of an occupying army was one thing; killing innocent countrymen another. Even though he gave it all up and joined the U.S. Army, his mother was lost to him.

True to form, O'Toole had quit the Army, too, after eighteen years of distinguished service, just short of retirement. He quit because he did not like being on a second-place team in the only sport he was any good at. Aside from drinking.

"Another Bushmill's," he told the bartender.

After his seventh double, O'Toole felt an overpowering sadness come upon him. There were many things an Irishman could lose and not care less about; his mother was not among them.

The booze flowed through his veins like lava, thick and molten. And then it began to speak to his soul.

A bit of verse popped into his head. Then another. And another. He had nothing to write it down with. And no real urge to scribble, anyway. As far as O'Toole was concerned, a poem was meant to be heard.

He put his back to the bar and addressed his fellow drinkers in a loud, clear baritone.

> "Tender mercy, tears of blood, anoint the guilty
> blameless bastard:
> Blunder headlong through the shambles,
> changed by fire, by smoke, by steel;
> changed by lives he has stolen."

The taciturn men looked up from their black brews and stared at him as if he was some kind of freak. One of them said, "Shut up."

O'Toole went on, undaunted. Listening to poetry was like kneeling in the confessional. It built character.

> "Like a creature made of mud,
> with twigs for fingers, stones for eyes:
> Blind thing staggering through the
> downpour..."

There were groans and muttered oaths all around.

"I said shut up," repeated a burly, grizzled man in a porkpie hat.

"Aye," said the man sharing the table with him, "let us drink in peace."

O'Toole was no longer thinking about meter and meaning. Nor his unwilling audience. He was only the conduit through which the words flowed. He did not notice the tall, white-haired man standing by the door.

> "Melting at each drop that pelts it;
> Melting from the sound of screams."

"I'll fix your screamin' hash," the burly man growled, shoving back his chair.

"And I'll help," said his mate. He cracked the neck off a Guinness bottle.

As they came at O'Toole the other drinkers shouted encouragement. The burly man lunged with his great paws stretched for the poet's throat. O'Toole shifted his weight and snap-kicked the man in the balls. With a gasp the fellow fell to his knees, put his forehead on the floor and started doing sea lion impressions.

His partner closed in with the broken bottle, feinting, jabbing at O'Toole's face. The red-haired man countered with some jabs of his own. Three straight, hard lefts snaked in over the man's guard. Each one landed flush, snapping his head back. O'Toole's right hand was cocked, ready, but it was not needed. The last jab took the man out. His legs buckled and he toppled, falling backward over his pal who was puking up stout by the pint.

O'Toole opened his mouth to continue his recitation only to discover that the words were gone. His muse, too, was lost. He turned back to the bar in disgust.

The white-haired man stepped over the fallen boozers and bellied up next to him. "You still got the gift, O'Toole," Barrabas said.

"Colonel! Damn, it's good to see you. A drink," he told the bartender. "A drink for the devil's own."

"Just one, for the road," Barrabas said. "We've got a job to do."

The Irishman gave him a crooked grin.

"Yeah, that's right," Barrabas said. "And this job you're gonna love."

THE ANDERS-CYCLONE WHINED FOR MERCY but Vince Biondi held it redlined at nine grand. In his peripheral view the fields and trees of rural Switzerland blurred into a solid wall of green. He was doing 210 miles per hour on the straight when the brake point leaped up at him. He downshifted and hit the third turn high and wide, his eyes locked on the groove, the six-inch-wide line on the roadway. It was not painted on; it was burned in, the rubber from tires of countless race cars making countless circuits of the Grand Prix track. It was the fastest line through the turn. It was also the safest line, assuming it was taken at the right speed.

Biondi was not interested in safety. There was one car ahead of him. One car to beat.

He took the 1.54g corner at 1.55g and could not hold the groove. The Formula One car's rear end came unstuck from the tarmac, skidding, slewing to the right, climbing up the bank toward the metal guardrail. For a split second he lost it altogether. Then precision-honed reflexes took over, compensating for the car's oversteer by a slight cut back in throttle. He barreled out of the turn, 550 horsepower pushing him.

Ahead, the taillights of the leader's red Ferrari flashed on as he braked for the dogleg-left coming up. Biondi lead-footed it, once again winding the big mill to redline. He pointedly ignored the engine's temperature gauge, which was creeping up into the danger zone.

At his last pit stop the owner of the car had warned him about the engine. "Come on, Vince, boy, don't push the machine so hard," he had said. "There's only fifteen laps to go. We can win this one if you lighten up. Let the Ferrari team make the mistakes. Just hang in there. You can do it."

Biondi had answered the man's patronizing concern in concise and graphic Italian. *"Va fan cullo."*

The owner of the Anders-Cyclone hated Biondi's guts. He was not alone. No owner on the

Formula One circuit could stand him. He drove the Grand Prix like it was a demolition derby. If the owners had had control over who got behind the wheel of their cars and who did not, Biondi would never have gotten another ride.

It was not the owners but the sponsors who called the shots. The only way an owner could hope to break even on his enormous investment was to lease out his vehicle. To turn it into a two-hundred-mile-an-hour billboard.

It had cost Brandon Cosmetics, Inc., a cool half million to get the name, logo and package color of their new men's cologne, Buckskin, on the Anders-Cyclone. It had cost Biondi his last thirty grand in corporate bribes to make sure he was selected to drive the tan-and-gold car.

Inside his matching, fire-resistant Nomex driving suit, Biondi was soaked with sweat. His arms and legs felt parboiled. He could have used some cologne, for sure.

Not Buckskin, though.

It smelled like a gay bathhouse on date night.

Through the switchbacks and hairpins Biondi picked up ground on the leader. By the time the two cars whipped through the last turn and shot into the long grandstand chute, they were dicing for the lead.

The Anders-Cyclone did not have enough power flat-out to beat the Ferrari on the straightaway. The driver of the red car cut in front of Biondi with inches to spare, then steadily crept away.

As they streaked past the grandstand Biondi saw the Anders-Cyclone pit crew frantically waving him in. The engine temperature gauge was almost pinned. Something was sour and it was getting worse. If he pulled in now they could probably fix whatever it was in time for him to get back into the race.

Probably.

If he played it safe, conservative, maybe the driver of the Ferrari would make a mistake and hand him the lead.

Maybe.

Probably and maybe were not good enough. Biondi had been eating Ferrari exhaust for 196 miles. He wanted the lead. Even though he was stuck in a slower car, he knew he could take it.

With perfect timing and solid-brass balls.

He flattened the accelerator, making the tach needle slice deep into the red, and somehow held the gap to four feet. He was looking at the Ferrari airfoil dead ahead, but seeing the track beyond in his mind. They were starting the next lap, going to turn one. He knew when the brake point was coming up for him. For the red car, he had to guess. At the same instant that the Ferrari's brake lights flashed on Biondi cut to the right. He swerved around the red car and zoomed past it. He had the lead, but he also had passed his own brake point. He swept into the turn going too fast for the groove.

Way too fast.

For a split second, it was okay. He rode the ragged edge, every nerve in his body supercharged as he fought the oversteer, the g-force. Halfway through, the rear tires broke loose and he was no longer battling another car; he was going one on one with the laws of physics. His reflexes overcorrected the trim. Then he lost it.

Everything blurred as the Anders-Cyclone spun counterclockwise down the track and into the guardrail. The machine jumped the barrier, cartwheeling end over end. It was flying apart around him.

Here it comes, Biondi thought. Shit!

He blacked out. When he came to, what was left of the car was sitting rightside up on the grass. Dense, oily smoke boiled up from the engine and blew over his back. He unsnapped his safety harness and struggled out of the form-fitting seat and then the high-sided driver's compartment. It was like a kid climbing out of a bathtub.

A burning bathtub.

He bailed out just in time. The methanol in the fuel tank ignited and the Anders-Cyclone went off like a napalm bomb.

Biondi tore off the tan-and-gold helmet and hurled it into the blaze. "Yeah, burn you pile of garbage!" he said.

The walk back to the pits was not a long one, but it was rough because his legs were rubbery in the knees. Nobody in the pit crew seemed glad to see him. The owner was disappointed that Biondi hadn't gone down with the ship.

"You'll never drive this circuit again!" the little man ranted. "I'll see to it! I swear to God!"

Biondi was looking over his shoulder, past him.

"What are you grinning at, asshole?" the owner said. "Hey, where the hell do you think you're going? I'm not through with you yet!"

Biondi walked away. Walked toward the two men who sat on the edge of the pit wall. One had red hair.

The other's was almost completely white.

5

Gunther Dykstra firmly pushed the woman in the stylishly hacked up red sweat shirt off his lap. She wore black satin pants so tight they looked like she'd need turpentine to remove them. Her hair was dyed robin's-egg blue. She was perfecting a petulant look.

"Later," he said, smacking her fondly on the bottom. "I have business with these guys."

Barrabas and Biondi half turned to follow the side-to-side swish of her exit with their eyes. Then Biondi said, "I've only got one question, Gunther."

The 260-pound blond Dutchman laughed. "Yeah, man, that's blue, too."

Barrabas looked out of the office's one-way window. Below was the Lido, Gunther's nightclub. He ran the place partly as a laundry for his smuggling profits and partly because he thoroughly enjoyed the club's atmosphere. A light show flickered and swirled on one wall; solitary dancers bopped to acid-rock cult favorites from the late sixties. The Lido was a hangout for psychedelic throwbacks, the odd punk rocker and tourists looking for some genuine but safe Dutch decadence. Gunther Dykstra was not and had never been a hippie, but the era and its milestones—sex, drugs and rock and roll—fascinated him.

"Have you thought about our little problem?" Barrabas asked.

The "little problem" was how to get the SOBs in and out of Iran alive.

"Yes and I've got the answer," Gunther said. "Tail-rotor gearboxes."

"Say what?" Biondi said.

Gunther's blue eyes twinkled. "I'm in a position to supply Iran with replacement tail-rotor gearboxes for their grounded Bell Cobra attack helicopters."

Biondi rolled his eyes, then addressed Barrabas. "This guy's had his nose in that blue fuzz too long. No way he can get hold of a shipment of restricted shit like that."

"Let him finish," Barrabas said.

"I have this friend in Taiwan," Gunther went on. "He specializes in counterfeiting aircraft parts."

The white-haired man frowned. "Iran has been burned before on a scam like that. They aren't going to be easy to fool."

"My friend and his associates do top-quality work," Gunther assured him. "Gearbox cases, serial numbers, magnaflux crack certification stamps—all will be perfect. Only what's inside the cases will be less than military spec.''

"And what if they decide to install a set of gears in one of their grounded birds and make us fly it?'' Biondi said.

"Fly? These gears won't even survive an engine warm-up. They'll be made of cheap, soft steel instead of high-temper moly. At a few thousand revs, ka-boom! And we'd better not be around when the pieces come down.''

"You can set up a black-market deal with the regime inside our time limit?'' Barrabas asked.

"Nile, these guys are going to fall all over themselves to get their hands on a hundred Cobra gearboxes.''

"A hundred?''

"Any fewer and they would be less anxious to deal. We want them drooling.''

Barrabas knew the Iranians were not the only ones with wet chins. "What do these gearboxes retail for on the open market?''

"About twenty-four grand apiece, but Iran will pay twice that and think they're stealing them. My Taiwanese friend already has a genuine gearbox to work from. He guarantees safe arrival of the parts in Bahrain in one week.''

"Jesus!'' Biondi exclaimed.

"If we were in Taiwan,'' Gunther told him, "this man could have a prototype of the finished product for us overnight.''

"He'll ship AOG?" Barrabas said.

"Yes, top priority, aircraft on ground," Gunther said. "The documentation will list them as parts for civilian agricultural helicopters."

"Yeah, Bahrain does a hell of a lot of crop dusting," Biondi quipped.

"Nobody will notice. A man at the bonded warehouse will help us get the shipment out of customs impound for a fat bribe."

"How much is your end of the operation going to set us back?" Barrabas asked. He had already guessed the answer.

"It will cost you nothing. I am financing all of it, myself."

"Yeah, out of the goodness of your heart," Barrabas said, grinning. "Gunther, you're going to make a killing on this. Four, maybe five million dollars, right?"

"I'll get half from them in advance," Gunther said. "The rest will be due upon delivery. I don't expect to collect the final payment."

"All this high finance is thrilling," Biondi said, "but what's the fucking game plan?"

"Real simple," Barrabas told him. "You and Gunther will make a chopper night flight with the Cobra parts from Bahrain to a delivery point in south-central Iran. After you unload the gearboxes, you'll head back to the coast. Everything will be on the up and up as far as the Iranian government is concerned. Your entrance and exit will be cleared in advance. The rest of the team will cross the Gulf in a smuggler's boat. You'll pick us and the battle gear up on the beach, take us to the LZ, then fly us out when the job's done."

"I'll tell you one thing," Biondi said, "we can't pull something like this off in a Huey. It doesn't have the range."

"That's right," Gunther said. "We'll be flying a Sikorsky S-76 Utility fitted with extended range tanks. I leased it from a small oil company in Bahrain. At two thousand dollars a day. A real bargain at only twice the going rate. If they knew what we were going to do with their baby, they wouldn't let us near it for any price."

"Yeah," Barrabas said, "a firestorm can really screw up a nice paint job."

6

William Starfoot II stared into a pair of black cesspools, the glittering eyes of his Aunt Thelma. She and the rest of the Talltree clan sat on the opposite side of the conference table, lined up like so many weather-beaten fence posts.

Whoever had come up with the name Talltree had been a real comedian. The Talltrees were all full-blooded Navajos—five by five. American Indian cubes. William Starfoot II, a.k.a. Billy Two, was only half Dineh, on his mother's side. Six foot six, broad-shouldered, lean-waisted, he took after his dad, an Osage from Oklahoma. Osage as in oil.

Billy Two's dad was one rich Indian.

The Talltrees were well-off, too, but there were a lot of them and they were all greedy.

Aunt Thelma's oldest son, Jarvis, stood up and addressed the Bureau of Indian Affairs lawyers and the handful of assembled Tribal Council delegates. "I assure you all that we're only trying to be practical in this," he said. "If we don't admit that Avarico Fuels has us whipped and give in, they're going to strip-mine the BLM property outside our tribal lands and the Nation will get nothing. No royalties. No jobs. We've got to grant them the lease they want.''

Billy Two smirked. Jarvis made it sound so logical, so inevitable. Never mind the fact that the Talltrees had a large stock interest in Avarico Fuels.

Aunt Thelma's narrow, wrinkled lips were moving, but she made no audible sound. The council delegate to Billy Two's left stiffened in his chair and jerked his gaze away from the old woman's.

Aunt Thelma was a Navajo witch. Back on the reservation she was a powerful presence. Bad things happened to those who opposed her. Folks fainted; their tongues turned black; they got lockjaw. Some died. It was said that Aunt Thelma could kill at long distance with a single pass of her hand.

Billy Two did not look away. He watched her dried-up lips squirm and pucker. The ''witchery way'' of the Navajo was linked with cannibalism, incest, fratricide and necrophilia. Billy Two could believe that Aunt Thelma had done all that, all on the same Saturday afternoon, but he could not believe she had any power, other than what stupid people let her take. He had suspected for a long time that she did not believe any of it herself, that her long-distance killing was accomplished with a little help from her sons and grandsons.

Jarvis sat down. The time for counterargument was now. Billy Two made no move to get up. He had not come to Washington, D.C., to argue. Everyone in the room knew about the Talltree-Avarico relationship. The strip-mine-lease proposal could be blocked at any one of the twenty steps required by Congress. The real problem was the Talltrees, specifically Aunt Thelma. Like a rattler, once she got her fangs into something tasty she never gave up. Someday she and her kin would succeed in pillaging the Navajo homeland, unless her power over the superstitious was checked.

It was time to fight fire with fire.

Billy Two casually tipped up the flap of his jean-jacket pocket and reached two fingers inside. What he fished out went straight into his mouth. As he smiled at Aunt Thelma the dry bean clicked against the back of his teeth. The Navajos believed that a wizard could hurt or kill an enemy by hitting him with a foreign particle, a spirit "arrow" in the form of a stone, a bone, a quill. A bean.

From his shirt pocket Billy Two took a plastic soda straw. He raised it to his lips.

Aunt Thelma's jaw went slack. She knew what was coming. Billy Two's cheeks puffed out and she could not move fast enough to escape. The hard bean smacked the old woman right between the eyes.

"What in the world!" one of the lawyers exclaimed.

Aunt Thelma sat there, momentarily stunned, not by the physical force of the blow, but by its meaning. It was an open challenge to her much-advertised supernatural powers.

"Grab him! Grab the bastard!" Jarvis shouted to the others.

No one made a move on Billy Two.

He slowly got up. Aunt Thelma was hopping mad. She had gotten the message, all right. And she knew the Tribal Council delegates would see to it the rest of the Nation got it, too.

"What is going on here?" the lawyer demanded.

"Meeting's adjourned," Billy Two said. He turned and walked out the door.

LIAM O'TOOLE DROVE straight from the D.C. airport to Billy Two's hotel. His orders from Barrabas were explicit: collect the troops in person, make sure there were no screwups, no missed planes, nobody drunk on arrival. As O'Toole stepped out of the elevator, a running man slammed into him, knocking him back against the doorframe. The man in the big hurry got the worst of the impact. He crashed to the carpet, belly first. Before O'Toole could shout "Hey, you!", the guy was up and sprinting for the fire stairs at the near end of the corridor. On the carpet he left behind a blue steel .38 revolver.

O'Toole bent down to pick it up.

"Leave it," said a voice at his back.

He straightened and slowly turned, keeping his hands in full view. A big brown man in underwear stood in the middle of the hall, opposite an open door. Cradled in his hands was a silenced, stainless-steel Smith and Wesson automatic.

"Billy? It's Liam," O'Toole said.

The man lowered his weapon. "In here," he said, stepping through the doorway.

O'Toole scooped up the .38 and trotted down the corridor. When he looked into the room he muttered an oath. The room reeked of cordite. It was decorated in Early Slaughterhouse.

Two dead men lay sprawled on the gold-and-white linoleum of the kitchenette, their chests blown open by concentrated pistol fire. On the balcony, beyond the open sliding glass door, a third man was curled up on his side. There were two dark holes in his forehead, one over each eye. The back of his skull was somewhere on the street, eight stories below.

"What was all this about?" O'Toole asked.

"Family squabble," Billy Two replied. He ejected the S&W's magazine, cleared the chamber of a live 9mm round and set the handgun on the kitchen counter. "The rough stuff was their idea, not mine."

A real bad idea, O'Toole thought. Four armed men had not managed to get off a single shot to their intended victim's thirteen. He watched the man pour himself a stiff drink of bourbon, then chug it down like tap water. "Barrabas sent me to get you," O'Toole said. "We've got a job."

Billy Two grimaced. "Yeah, well, I've got kind of a mess on my hands. A hard-to-explain mess."

"So, don't explain it," O'Toole told him. "Let me go get some plastic tarps, then we'll clean up here."

"And them?" Billy Two asked, indicating the fallen Talltrees with a nod of his head.

"Fish food."

NATE BECK thought he had died and gone to heaven.

Sure, it was only a volleyball game he was watching. Sure, the players were terrible. But they were young, good-looking and female.

They were also gloriously, unabashedly topless.

"What's the score, now?" the man on the canvas beach chair to his right asked.

The guy on the other side of Beck answered. "Don't know. Can't seem to concentrate on the ball. Why don't you go ask 'em?"

"Yeah, I think I will."

"Nanos, you don't speak French," Nate said.

The Greek was already up and moving. He glanced back over his shoulder. As he did, suntan-oil-lubed lats and traps bulged. "This body speaks all languages," he said, flashing brilliant white teeth.

"Whew, old Alex does think mighty highly of himself," Wiley Drew Boone said as the bronzed man cut across the sand in the direction of the volleyball court. "But he'll never pull it off alone."

"Pull what off?" Beck said.

Boone sat up and slung a towel around his neck. "Arrange it so this afternoon the three of us sleep with the six of them. You just lay there, Nate. Save your strength. You're gonna need it." With that he hurried to catch up with the Greek.

Nate Beck sank back in the canvas chair. The time since the last mission had passed like a dream. He, Nanos and Boone had spent their earnings for the Kaluba job in one week. Fifty grand apiece. It was a hell of a week, though. First Paris, then the Riviera. The casinos had really chewed up their dough. Boone had had to call the States and ask his multimillionaire father for an advance on his monthly allowance to cover the gambling debts they had run up. Then Beck had gotten his baccarat system together. The computer wizard had hit the casinos so hard they barred him from play. He had tried to teach the system to Nanos and Boone, but they did not have his knack with numbers.

Across the stretch of sand, the two of them

stood by the net post. The French girls stopped their game in midvolley, breaking into peals of laughter. Boone was grinning and Nanos gesturing animatedly with both hands.

No, they had a different knack and a different set of numbers.

When Nate Beck was a skinny little Jewish boy he had had a recurring fantasy. He was running buddies with Errol Flynn and John Wayne. Every day after Hebrew school, the three of them prowled the dusty Western streets, the grim Macao back alleys, the teeming African jungles of his imagination, looking for wrongs to right. Nanos and Boone were not Flynn and Wayne. They were a man's fantasy, not a boy's. Real edge-of-hell guys. Uncensored. Genuine soldiers of fortune, too raw, too rugged for the screen.

And Nate Beck, now a skinny little Jewish man, was one of them. A swashbuckler. A mercenary.

He had never felt so great in his whole life.

Or so guilty.

A few weeks before he had been recruited by Barrabas, Beck had been in freefall. Bored by the easy success of his computer company, the tedium of a marriage gone stale, he had decided to change his life with one bold stroke. He had turned his astronomical IQ to crime. Computer crime. He had programmed his firm's computers to siyphon off a million dollars and pump it into a dummy Swiss account. It had run like clockwork till the cuckoo emerged. His wife, Beverly, had ratted on him. Nate Beck was an international fugitive, but that was not what was making him feel so lousy about feeling so good.

Even as Nanos and Boone waved at him to join them at courtside, a voice in his head told him, sure, go ahead, you heartless schmuck, have your slimeball fun, screw the little schicksas' brains out, worry your poor mother sick.

Beck had not called home since he had gone on the run. At first he had been too busy with the SOBs. Then he had rationalized his silence by telling himself it was too dangerous. The phone lines were undoubtedly tapped. But deep down he was less paranoid about the FBI than he was about what his mother would say to her son, the criminal.

"Aw, dammit to hell," he said, groaning. The longer he put it off, the more difficult it would get. He cupped his hands and shouted to Nanos and Boone, "Back in a minute!"

He pulled on his T-shirt, stepped into his sandals and headed for the hotel lobby. He spoke to the desk clerk, arranging for the overseas charges to be added to his bill, then found an empty phonebooth. He took off his wristwatch, put it where he could see it, and dialed. As soon as the receiver was picked up at the other end, he started the elapsed-time function on the watch.

"Hello?" said a familiar voice.

"Ma, it's Nathan."

There was a pause. A long pause. He shut his eyes tight.

"Nathan," his mother said, "are you all right?"

"Yes, ma."

"Are you eating?"

"Yes, ma."

"I don't believe you. I have pencil and paper. Give me your address. I'll send you a little something."

"I can't, ma. I'm sorry."

Beck strained to hear the telltale click of the wiretap. There was too much static on the line for him to be sure.

"You're okay, ma?"

"I'm doing as well as can be expected."

The dig was only half-hearted. That made it all the worse. She still loved him, in spite of everything.

"Look, I've got to go now," he said. His vision was blurred by tears; he could no longer see the watch face. "I love you, ma."

He did not wait for her reply. He hung up. For a minute or two he just stood there, looking at the wall.

A sharp knock on the window of the phone-booth brought him back to reality. Some impatient asshole wanted to use the phone. Beck turned and stared into the beaming face of Liam O'Toole.

7

Nile Barrabas stood in the deep shade of Casa Hatton's vine-draped veranda, looking downhill. Between neat rows of fig and almond trees the corrugated metal roof of the bunkhouse reflected the blazing midday sun. A line of men in fatigues straggled from the bunkhouse, up the winding gravel path toward him. In the dead-still air their wisecracks and laughter carried all the way to the ranch house.

The ranch, or *estancia*, was on the Spanish island of Málaga, its grounds backed up against the jagged ridge of mountains known as La Serra. The area was rugged and remote and the authorities who patrolled it were dismally underpaid. It was an ideal training base for a private army.

"They sure sound in good spirits," said a female voice behind him.

Even without makeup, in a baggy fatigue shirt and cutoff fatigue pants, the owner of the ranch was one beautiful woman. Pale-skinned, black-eyed Dr. Leona Hatton wore her hair cut very short. It was the color of a raven's wing.

"Yeah," Barrabas said, "they don't know what they're in for, yet."

As the mercenaries filed past Dr. Hatton and into the ranch house, not one of them said a lewd or suggestive word.

Lee Hatton was an expert in Escrima, the Filipino art of self-defense. With stick, knife or hands and feet, she was more than a match for any of them. She was also one hell of a combat doctor.

Barrabas was the last to enter the house. It was cool inside, thanks to thick brick and plaster walls and tile floors. The place was centuries old and looked it. It had been a restoration project that Lee's father, a retired general and former OSS man, never lived to complete. She had inherited the antiques, the paintings, the worn Catalan rugs, along with the dry rot, the leaky roof and the fallen ceilings. Gamely she was tackling the enormous job of putting the house back in shape.

Barrabas followed her and the men into the casa's main dining room where O'Toole had set up the visuals for the preliminary briefing.

Nanos, Billy Two, Boone and Beck sat at one side of the long table, Biondi, Hatton, Hayes and Chen on the other. Claude Hayes, the only black on the team, was a former underwater-demolition man, quiet, full of inner strength, a real contrast to his jiving, womanizing counterparts on the squad. Al Chen, the only Oriental, was definitely one of the boys. The one-time Olympic-class gymnast was an Air Force vet, a balloonist, hang-glider pilot and skydiver.

Everyone in the room, with the notable exception of Dr. Lee Hatton, was an NCO. That was not a term of rank. It was combat slang, meaning they had absolutely "no chance outside" the military. Barrabas smiled. Some of them did not even stand a chance inside it. They were all different, came from different ethnic and social backgrounds, but they had that common link—a streak of wildness that bordered on self-destruction.

When Jessup and Barrabas had gone over the personnel for the first mission, the Texan had warned him specifically about two candidates. Nanos and Billy Two. A pair of funny men with a track record of pulling hare brained get-rich-quick schemes that usually involved wealthy women and endurance humping.

The colonel could go right down the list and pick out some serious flaw in all of them. O'Toole drank way too much. Boone was a fool for women. Beck was too small. And Biondi, Christ, he was almost certifiable.

Barrabas was not their keeper or their judge. There were fine cracks in him, too. He was the force that made them mesh, that made all the weak spots compensate for each other, that made them a team.

He stepped to the head of the table. "You've

probably all noticed that we're missing somebody. Lopez wanted to come along, but Dr. Hatton said no way. He's still recovering from the
wounds he got in Kaluba.''

The troops were silent. Only transfusions of
their blood and the skill of Lee Hatton had kept
their buddy from buying the farm in Africa.

''Before I get into the specifics of the mission,'' Barrabas said, ''I want to talk money.''

There were smiles all around.

''This job is going to pay two hundred grand
per man.''

Billy Two broke the stunned silence with a
piercing war whoop. The rest of the mercenaries
joined in, laughing, slapping the tabletop.

Only Claude Hayes kept his cool. ''What do
we have to do?'' he asked.

Barrabas answered in two words.

''Nuke Iran.''

The silence was much longer this time. The
SOBs knew their white-haired leader had not
dragged them halfway around the world to make
a joke.

Barrabas took the pointer from O'Toole and
jabbed its tip at the blownup satellite recon
photos tacked to the blackboard. ''This is our
target,'' he said. ''An atomic-weapons-research-
and-development lab in south-central Iran. It
now holds four nuclear bombs in the thirty-
kiloton class. The site's protected by seventy-five
to one hundred Islamic Revolutionary Guards.

Our job is to isolate the site by cutting radio links, to penetrate and negate the guard force and to detonate one of the weapons in place, destroying everything and everyone there.''

"Holy shit," Nanos muttered.

"That's right, Alex. We're going to have to earn our money this time. Seventy-five percent of the research complex is underground in a system of bunkers. Liam will give you the breakdown of the site's permanent defenses.''

He passed the pointer back to O'Toole and sat down.

"What we have here on the surface, gentlemen,'' the Irishman said, "is pretty typical of any nuclear-weapons storage facility. The perimeter is triple fenced, probably with electrified wire. There are floodlights along the top of the fence and on top of these four guard towers. There's only one road in and out. It's dirt and it winds south and east, over a ridge of low mountains. Eventually it connects with the main road south to Bandar-e 'Abbās and the Persian Gulf. This whole area, if you're not familiar with it, is a wasteland, uninhabited except for a few tiny oases.''

He pointed out two spots on the largest of the recon photos. "Outside the wire, on this broad plain, we've got a pair of listening posts, each with its own set of noise detectors. The radio tower that links the site with the military base at Kerman is on top of the easternmost of the two peaks that wall off the rear of the compound. Each peak has its own guard post.''

O'Toole drew the tip of the pointer down the mountain slope, over the saddle that connected the two peaks, to a rectangle bracketed by what looked like sandbags. ''This is the entrance to the bunker system, which cuts back into the saddle. What they did here was to partially excavate, building floors and walls slightly below ground level. After they put on the ceilings and roof they used bulldozers and dynamite to collapse the sides of the mountains and saddle, burying the complex under thousands of tons of rock and dirt. As far as conventional weapons go, it's bombproof. And it would survive anything less than a direct hit with a nuclear warhead.''

O'Toole tacked another, much larger blowup over the recon photos; it was of a crude, hand-drawn map. ''This was sketched from memory by a man on the inside at the site. It's all the information we've got on the underground floorplan. As you can see, there are four distinct work areas: an electronics lab, a high-explosives assembly and storage room, a large metal shop and the radioactive-materials lab. All four are in the most deeply buried part of the bunker. In the front, near the entrance, are the dormitory, the armory and the mess hall. We're going to have to go through them to get to our objective.''

''What do those zigzag lines mean?'' Beck asked.

"Good question. Those indicate the connecting corridors between rooms. They zigzag just like that. And for a good reason. Radiation, X rays, gamma rays and neutrons all travel in straight lines. The zigzagging helps deflect and stop radioactive particles in case of an accident."

"Ouch!" Nanos said, jamming both hands under the table, covering his crotch.

O'Toole's blue eyes twinkled. "Alex, the 'accident' we're going to cause is going to blow a hole in that plain a half mile wide. Your crotch is the least of your worries."

"Not in his case," Billy Two said. "It's where his brains are."

"Our opposition," O'Toole went on, "are troops seasoned in the border war with Iraq. Not regular army, but Pasdaran, which means they've each had a six-month brainwashing in the ideology of the Islamic Republic. They're fanatically loyal to the regime. They'll be armed with Heckler and Koch G-3 assault rifles, Uzis, Iranian copies of Soviet PPSH-41 sub and Czech ZB-30 light machine guns, frag and concussion grenades."

"How are we going to take these wildmen out?" Chen asked.

Heads nodded around the table.

"We don't have to kill them all," O'Toole said. "What we have to do is drive them back, into the hindmost part of the bunker and pin them down there while we rig the bomb to explode. We figure roughly one-third of the guard force will be on duty aboveground, outside the bunker, when we hit the site at about 0200 hours. We have to eliminate the troops outside, then get to and through the entrance before they can close the double steel doors. If we don't make it, it's going to be a long night. The further we can penetrate the complex before they wise up, the easier it's going to be to gain our objective.''

He looked around the room. "Any questions?''

There were none. But there were some mighty sober faces.

"Good,'' he said. "Tonight you're all going to get a refresher course in the use of the Starlite nightscope, then, while it's still dark, we're going to go climb us a few mountains.''

8

Billy Two pressed his right eye tight to the Star-lite scope's rubber cup and peered into the sight. Everything on the other side of the cross hairs was ghostly, shades of yellow, yellow-green and green. It was a trick of fiber optics, picking up the weak starlight reflected off the surfaces of objects, then enhancing it so a clear image emerged. A clear image of rocks, rocks and more rocks as he slowly scanned the south face of one of La Serra's rugged slopes.

The last time Billy Two had had his hands on a Starlite sniperscope was when he was a Marine commando in Vietnam. He had thought then that it would make a great prop for a spy movie. As a military tool in a jungle war it was not worth shit. The only way to pick out a still target with a Starlite scope was to find the human out-line, the shape of a head, a shoulder or the like. In Nam the vines, trees and brush broke up out-lines.

The terrain he was working with now was much easier to read. It reminded him of parts of the Navajo homeland. He swept the sight past a crevice between two large rocks, then brought it back. The head shape was there, in the notch. He pulled the M-21 rifle tight to his shoulder. It was a special version of the M-14, tailored for sniper use, chambered for 7.62mm NATO round. This particular M-21 was equipped with a bipod and a Sionics Noise Suppressor. Billy laid the cross hairs in the middle of his target and tightened down on the trigger. The rifle bucked, its report an indistinct pop.

Thanks to the suppressor, the scope's picture was not overloaded and wiped out by the muzzle-flash. That had been another problem in Nam. It had turned sniping into a one-shot-and-duck deal. The shooter had to wait for the scope and his vision to recover from the flash before he could follow up the first bullet. By that time his target was gone. Or angry.

His target, a man-sized dummy, jerked back from its hiding place and slumped over, its exploded head hanging in tatters.

"Nice shooting," O'Toole said, turning away from the Starlite spotting scope.

"This gizmo works real good," Billy Two observed. "Like to take one of these home after the mission is over."

"A little deer after dark?"

"No. Back home I've got some varmints to take care of."

"Varmints, huh?"

"Yeah, the red-faced kind."

ALEX NANOS dragged himself up onto the narrow ledge, then sat with the back of his pack hard against the rock wall and his legs dangling off into nothingness. Four nights of humping over steep, broken ground, of free-climbing three-thousand-foot peaks in full pack and weapons, was getting to him. He knew it was necessary for the mission, but that did not make it fun.

Nothing could make cuts, scrapes, bruises and muscle strains fun.

"Need some help, Nanos?" Lee said as she scrambled up beside him.

She was not even breathing hard.

"No, I'm fine," he lied.

The turnabout was startling. On the first mission it had been the lady doctor who had had trouble with the physical load required of a foot soldier. She had gutted it out, though. And she had not let down after the Kaluba job was over. She had been doing hard farm and construction work. As a result, she was in better condition than the Greek, despite all his showy bulges. The only muscle Nanos had diligently exercised during the layoff was of no use to him now.

"Do you mind if I pass you?" the doctor asked.

"No," he said, telling another lie. "Go right ahead."

Then and there Alex Nanos swore off booze and bimbos forever.

And this time he was pretty sure he meant it.

"IT'S GOING TO BE a piece of cake," Nate Beck told Barrabas as they walked down the casa's sparsely furnished hallway. The computer-and-electronics genius had solved the problem of detonating the nuclear device. "The key to a weapon of this type is the trigger. A sphere of chemical explosive implodes, compressing the plutonium and starting the fission chain reaction. This lab has to have a test area for trying out the design of the implosion devices it develops. They would run a set of wires from the device, a couple of hundred yards off on the plain, back to the bunker and then detonate from there. All we have to do is rig their test system to a completed bomb."

"And the timer?" Barrabas asked.

"No problem. I'll bring something I can jerry-rig on the spot. A soldering iron, wire cutters and some tape is all I'm going to need."

It was all coming together. Barrabas could feel it. The SOBs had shaken off the cobwebs they had accumulated during the layoff. They were back in fighting form. Sharp. Quick. Deadly. Even Nanos had pulled himself together. And in the colonel's veins the old magic was flowing, as well. He had that exhilarating sense of purpose, of impending confrontation. They were rushing toward a test of will, all of them.

The ultimate pop quiz.

They entered the main dining room, where the rest of the SOBs were already seated. Dr. Hatton had the floor.

"Now that we're all here," she said, "the colonel has asked me to outline for you some of the medical hazards of this particular job."

"Aside from a hundred fanatics armed with Uzis and G-3s?" Chen asked.

"That's right. I'm going to talk about radiation. First of all, the rad lab inside the bunker is going to have a hot box—a sealed, protective container in which nuclear material can be safely handled with some kind of mechanical gripping apparatus. If this case gets ruptured and there's plutonium inside, any prolonged exposure will mean death in a matter of hours or days. Each of us will wear a dosimeter, which will keep track of the total dose of rems we receive—after the fact. Too late to do anything about it.

"Another danger for us is the actual nuclear explosion. There are four main components to it. First is the physical blast, which includes a shock wave and an overpressure zone. The shock wave will be traveling at roughly nine thousand miles per hour. It can pick up large and small objects and punch them right through you. And vice versa. The overpressure zone will produce more than twelve pounds of pressure per square inch. Enough to crush a car flat.

"The second component is thermal or heat. At the hypocenter of the blast the temperature will reach 300,000 degrees Celsius.

"Thirdly, right after the explosion there is a burst of 'prompt radiation,' X rays, gamma rays, neutrons, which usually extends well beyond the actual blast radius.

"Finally, there is fallout. Fragments of radioactive material blown into the air."

"The other bombs won't go off?" Nanos asked.

"No. But thanks to the plutonium, it's going to be a long time before anyone goes near the research site again."

"Yeah, say fifty years," Beck said.

"Back to the hazards. The effects of prompt radiation and fallout aren't immediately visible or apparent. The effects of blast and thermal radiation are. Claude, cut the lights and turn on the projector."

When the black-and-white slide popped onto the screen a shudder passed through the audience of hard-bitten mercenaries. The charred mass pictured was barely recognizable as human, but it was definitely alive. Its mouth gaped in a silent scream.

"At one and a half miles from the hypocenter of the explosion," Dr. Hatton said, "flash burn will carbonize skin and flesh. Next slide."

It showed a middle-aged Japanese woman from the neck up. The skin of her face hung from her chin like a Halloween mask. "This is the result of thermal burn. It has cooked the outer layers of skin and made them slough. This can be expected at two and a half miles from hypocenter."

"And how far away are we going to be?" Biondi asked.

"If everything goes as planned, we should be twenty miles from ground zero at detonation. Far enough away to miss the effects I've discussed."

"And if something goes wrong?" Nanos said.

Dr. Hatton did not answer.

Hayes's voice cut through the silence of the darkened room. "If something goes wrong," he said, "we'll *all* be black."

9

Mohamadi Razod stared at the completed nuclear device, a righteous sneer on his lips. The bomb was dull silver in color, a sphere slightly larger than a basketball, its outer surface studded like a cactus with detonators. To Razod it was nothing less than the false god of the idolatrous West. The ultimate yardstick of strength and importance among the world's oppressors. He did not understand the operating principles of the weapon before him. And he was proud of his ignorance of such matters.

As Razod watched, a group of scientists wheeled in the bomb's shock- and waterproof metal housing, a cylinder five feet long and three feet in diameter.

"How much longer?" he demanded of the project's senior scientist.

Dr. Hamid mopped his brow with a linen handkerchief. He was perspiring heavily; there were wet rings under the armpits of his lab coat. "We only have to install the weapon in its protective casing, connect the detonators to the timing device and set the automatic-destruct, antitamper switches."

"How much longer?"

"Three or four hours."

Razod scowled. With these scientists everything always took longer than it was supposed to. If he had not started them working around the clock in eighteen-hour shifts, they would never have completed one bomb, let alone four. It was typical of the soft, weak educated classes, used to easy jobs behind desks, pushing around pieces of paper. Jobs that paid much money. Razod looked at Dr. Hamid's haggard face and felt a warmth touch his heart. This job they were doing free, out of their love for their God and His holy nation. It was fitting that it be the hardest work of their lives.

"Do it in two," Razod said. "And get some men started crating up one of the completed bombs. We move it to the coast tomorrow night."

The captain of the Pasdaran was not interested in Dr. Hamid's feeble protests. He turned his back on the man and left the rad lab. At the door he headed right, down the corridor, toward his quarters. His path weaved back and forth between the floor-to-ceiling piles of sandbags that blocked alternate sides of the hallway, creating a zigzag effect.

When he reached the doorway of his quarters he stopped a passing soldier and said, "Send Lieutenant Yazdi to me at once."

As the Pasdar rushed off, Razod entered his

room. It was very small, barely six feet wide, and had Spartan furnishings: a folding cot and blanket; a writing table; a mirror on the wall and beside it a large poster of the bearded, wild-eyed man who was Razod's spiritual and political leader.

The captain sat on the edge of the cot and took a book from the small table. It was a holy work, written by the man who gazed down at him from the wall. He did not open it, but held it between his hands. There was power in the book, the power of God. It had proven itself stronger than the silver sphere. And soon it would turn the silver idol against its worshipers.

The first weapon was to be moved by truck convoy south to the Persian Gulf. There it would be loaded as regular cargo on a freighter destined for Haifa. While the first bomb was clearing the Suez Canal, the other weapons would be moved to their designated targets around the world. Targets much easier to hit than Israel.

The Pasdars had no hope of getting their deadly cargo ashore at Haifa. They had no intention of trying. Once the freighter was safely anchored in the harbor, but before it was boarded by Israeli customs inspectors, a Pasdar posing as a seaman would engage the detonation timer.

How could a nuclear blast a mile out to sea damage the state of Israel? Razod was ignorant of the science that made the device work, but he was knowledgeable about its effects. An enormous radioactive steam cloud would be thrown up by the blast. It would drift eastward over the coast of Israel, dropping the rain of terrible vengeance.

Israel would not dare retaliate. Not after the Government of God announced that there were more bombs in place, ready to be exploded at the first sign of a counterattack. Bombs that would take out civilian population centers inside the borders of Israel's Western allies. Iran would humiliate the Jewish state as it had humiliated America, before the entire world. The atomic blast would be a rallying point for all the oppressed nations of Islam. Together they would crush and expel their enemies.

External and internal.

Some of those enemies were very close at hand.

Dr. Hamid and the other scientists might have considered themselves to be patriots, but Razod knew better. They represented a grave danger to their country. They had intimate knowledge of the nuclear project. And unlike the Pasdars at the site, they were corrupted by Western humanism and materialism, either of which could lead to a fatal breach of security before the weapons were in place. It had been clear to Razod from the very start that as soon as their work on the project was completed, the scientists had to be dealt with swiftly and efficiently.

The idea appealed to Razod very much. He

was at his best, a man of iron, when he was crushing the enemies of God. He recalled with great pleasure his role in Operation Fathelfotuh, the battle of Bostan. It had been his inspired idea to use captured Iraqi prisoners of war to clear the mine fields that blocked the Pasdaran advance. Those prisoners who had not willingly walked forward had been shot on the spot. And each time an Iraqi located a mine with feet, hands, knees, each time one exploded, throwing a cloud of dirt and shredded flesh into the air, the Islamic Revolutionary Guards sent up a cheer in praise of Allah.

"Come," he said in answer to a knock on the door.

Lieutenant Yazdi entered. "You sent for me, sir?"

Razod leaned his back against the cement wall and put a boot up on the edge of the cot. "I will be supervising the transport of the first weapon to Bandar-e 'Abbās," he said. "In my absence you will, of course, take command here."

"Thank you, sir."

"I have a special order I want you to carry out while I am gone."

Yazdi nodded.

"After the fourth bomb has been assembled," he said, "quick-march all the scientists out onto the plain and shoot them. Give them absolutely no explanation, do you understand?"

"Yes, sir."

Razod smiled. It was a pity that he could not be present at the executions, but there was a bright side. The pure illogic of being summarily shot in the absence of the camp commander, apparently on the whim of a junior officer, would make the scholars' final moments all the more terrible.

DR. HAMID PUSHED his fellow scientists aside and leaned over the coffin-shaped bomb housing. "What is the trouble now?" he asked.

"The weapon's support brackets don't fit," the man next to him said. "They need to be re-machined."

"Is that a matter for debate?" he snapped. "Don't talk about it, fix it!"

The crowd of men in white scattered.

Hamid groaned inwardly. He knew what the real problem was. Exhaustion. They had been getting too little sleep for too long. And the pressure they were working under was unbearable. Every few hours Captain Razod would break in on them and demand a progress report. As a result, they were all making mistakes—stupid mistakes, over and over. At the rate they were moving now, it would take them twenty hours instead of two to get the weapon system assembled.

He walked back to his cluttered desk and sat down on the hard chair. His hands trembled uncontrollably in his lap. The quaking did not start there; it started at the core of him. It felt as if his whole body was about to fly apart.

If the others had been managing three or four hours of sleep over the past weeks, they had been doing much better than he had. Since the death of Dr. al-Barani he had been having awful dreams. No sooner would he close his eyes and begin to drift off than he would see his old friend on the unlit pyre, see the burning match in his own shaking fingers. At the moment in dream when the gasoline ignited, Dr. Hamid would lurch bolt upright in bed, gasping for air, dripping with cold sweat.

Awake he could mold the memory of what he had done.

When it came to rationalizing, Hamid was among the truly gifted.

He had convinced himself that though he had caused the "accident" that roasted his comrade, he had not murdered the man. al-Barani had taken his own life. There could be no question of that. If Hamid had any guilt to bear it was over the fact that he had not done something to help al-Barani weeks before, when he first started to act strangely.

But there was rationale for that, too.

The sudden change in the astrophysicist had frightened Hamid. You did not question the goals of a project as important as this. Certainly you did not suggest a mutiny to put an end to it. Not if you wanted to go on living.

A terrible choice had to be made. And Hamid had made it. He had turned his old friend in to the Pasdaran. If word of al-Barani's derangement had leaked out to them, word that Hamid had known about it and had said nothing, there would have been two bodies in the fire instead of one. The brutal torture brought on by the betrayal again was not Hamid's fault. He had not told Razod to break the man's legs. He had not told al-Barani to go crazy, either.

None of it was his responsibility.

Dr. Hamid had one burning ambition: to keep on breathing. That single-minded purpose, and the logic used to achieve it, brooked no interference. It smothered whatever feeble excuse for a conscience he might have possessed. It far outweighed his religious and patriotic zeal. It allowed him to build weapons for the slaughter and maiming of innocents. The inevitable results of dense nuclear fallout over populated areas were no mystery to him. He knew all about the radiation sickness, leukemia, gross deformities in the unborn, future cancers. He knew and he did not give a damn.

10

Liam O'Toole and Wiley Drew Boone sat at the bar of the American-run Club Sakr, nursing a couple of beers gone flat, watching long legs scissor past as the live entertainment danced nude along the bar top.

Liam groaned into his beer glass. "Damn, that is one wonderful rump," he said.

"Miraculous," Wiley Drew Boone agreed.

The dancer was blond all over, as were the four girls in the band. O'Toole could see them in the reflection of the mirror behind the bar, bopping, mugging, having what appeared to be the time of their lives as they delivered a very thin rendition of a current American Top 40 favorite.

"Can you imagine playing rock and roll in the buff?" O'Toole said.

"Not me, personally."

"I mean, when you think about it, it makes about as much sense as having a female stand-up comic do her bits naked."

Boone turned on the well-padded stool and looked around the dimly lit room. "When it comes to naked bits, this part of the world is Deprivation City.''

O'Toole turned and looked, too. The airport club was typical Bahrain. That is to say, it might as well have been Las Vegas or Atlantic City. The number of men dressed in traditional white headdresses and robes would not have been out of place even in Beverly Hills. They were Saudis and Kuwaitis who had come to the island in the Persian Gulf to sample some of the more minor vices of the West: booze and naked blondes. Things that were taboo in their strict Muslim countries.

Bahrain had done well for itself, considering it had no oil reserves of its own and was not much more than a salt marsh. It was surrounded by neighbors who needed basic services, banking and recreation, and were willing and able to pay through the nose for them.

The airports of the Middle Eastern countries O'Toole had previously visited had been like Wild West gold-rush towns. Nearly everybody packed a piece right up front. Not six-shooters but Makarovs. And when there was a power failure at night it was the signal for a blaze of gunfire in the darkened corridors, an opportunity for feuding parties to strike and slip away.

In Bahrain there were no gunslingers. Compared to say, Yemen, Bahrain was Disneyland.

O'Toole checked his watch. The flight from

1. How do you rate _____ ?
   (Please print book TITLE)

   1.6 ☐ excellent   .4 ☐ good   .2 ☐ not so good
   .5 ☐ very good   .3 ☐ fair   .1 ☐ poor

2. How likely are you to purchase another book in this series?
   2.1 ☐ definitely would purchase   .3 ☐ probably would not purchase
   .2 ☐ probably would purchase   .4 ☐ definitely would not purchase

   W 1 2 3 4 5

3. How do you compare this book with similar books you usually read?
   3.1 ☐ far better than others   .4 ☐ not as good
   .2 ☐ better than others   .5 ☐ definitely not as good
   .3 ☐ about the same

4. Have you any additional comments about this book?
   _____ (4)
   _____ (6)

5. How did you *first* become aware of this book?
   8. ☐ read other books in series   11. ☐ friend's recommendation
   9. ☐ in-store display   12. ☐ ad inside other books
   10. ☐ TV, radio or magazine ad   13. ☐ other _____
   (please specify)

6. What *most* prompted you to buy this book?
   14. ☐ read other books in series   17. ☐ title   20. ☐ story outline on back
   15. ☐ friend's recommendation   18. ☐ author   21. ☐ read a few pages
   16. ☐ picture on cover   19. ☐ advertising   22. ☐ other
   (please specify)

7. Have you purchased any books from any of these series or by these authors in the past 12 months? Approximately how many?

	No. Purchased		No. Purchased
☐ Mack Bolan	(23) ____	☐ Clive Cussler	(49) ____
☐ Able Team	(25) ____	☐ Len Deighton	(51) ____
☐ Phoenix Force	(27) ____	☐ Ken Follet	(53) ____
☐ SOBs	(29) ____	☐ Colin Forbes	(55) ____
☐ Dagger	(31) ____	☐ Frederick Forsyth	(57) ____
☐ The Destroyer	(33) ____	☐ Adam Hall	(59) ____
☐ Death Merchant	(35) ____	☐ Jack Higgins	(61) ____
☐ The Mercenary	(37) ____	☐ Gregory MacDonald	(63) ____
☐ Casca	(39) ____	☐ John D. MacDonald	(65) ____
☐ Nick Carter	(41) ____	☐ Robert Ludlum	(67) ____
☐ The Survivalist	(43) ____	☐ Alistair MacLean	(69) ____
☐ Duncan Kyle	(45) ____	☐ John Gardner	(71) ____
☐ Stephen King	(47) ____	☐ Helen McInnes	(72) ____

8. On which date was this book purchased? (75) _____

9. Please indicate your age group and sex.
   77.1 ☐ Male   78.1 ☐ under 15   .3 ☐ 25-34   .5 ☐ 50-64
   .2 ☐ Female   .2 ☐ 15-24   .4 ☐ 35-49   .6 ☐ 65 or older

Thank you for completing and returning this questionnaire.

Madrid was more than an hour late. Even so, they had plenty of time to spare. All but three of the SOBs were already in Bahrain. The last to arrive would be Lee, Beck and Billy Two. Gunther and Biondi had been on the island the longest. They had arranged for the release of the counterfeit Cobra parts and the team's weapons' cache from the bonded warehouse. The parts were already loaded on the leased Sikorsky chopper. The only missing piece of the plan was the boat that would take them across the Gulf. Barrabas, Hayes and Nanos were seeing to that right now.

Before they had left Málaga, O'Toole and Boone had both gotten all their affairs in order. The Irishman had made his mother the sole beneficiary of the large life-insurance policy the colonel had taken out for him. He had also arranged for the money in a six-figures bank account to go to a brother in Chicago, with the stipulation that it be distributed equally to the rest of the O'Toole clan. They were not as touchy as his mother when it came to "blood money."

As for Boone, O'Toole knew for a fact that he had assigned his insurance to a Mrs. Florence De Long of Atlanta, Georgia, the madam of what he called "the finest house of ill repute in the Western Hemisphere."

On that subject, the man's opinion had to be respected.

O'Toole glanced at Boone. He was a playboy, all right. A rich kid screwup. But he was also willing to put his butt on the line. Not for the money; his father had twenty-five million. Not for the glory, either. If this mission went off right, no one would ever know they were in on it. If it went wrong, they would take the heat. Maybe at 300,000 degrees Celsius.

Some of the other guys on the team were better soldiers, more coordinated, sharper with weapons. But Boone made up for all that with raw nerve. He was the kind of guy who needed to test that nerve every so often.

Like O'Toole and the others, Wiley Drew Boone believed that what was not worth a risk was not worth having.

BARRABAS ROLLED the perfectly matched pair of black pearls around in his palm. Then he took each one and rubbed it against his front tooth, trying to find the grittiness that would tell him they were genuine. They were heavy, gem-quality product, all right, typical of Bahrain's once world-famous oyster beds but particularly rare since pollution had virtually finished off the overfished beds in the Persian Gulf. He imagined what they would look like against Erika's smooth skin. Ebony on white satin. People used to believe pearls grew in the brains of dragons. A perfect gift, thought Barrabas. Yeah, they would make a damn fine pair of earrings. He nodded to the man behind the counter and reached into his front trouser pocket. He pulled out a rubber-banded wad of money inches thick and tossed it onto the glass counter top.

"Fifteen thousand dollars," he said.

The merchant riffled through the stack of hundreds with the dexterity of a bank clerk. When he finished, he was all smiles. "Would you like them boxed, sir?" he said.

"I want them sent," Barrabas said, taking a business card out of his shirt pocket. He turned the card over and wrote the letter *B* on the back, then handed it to the man. "By air to this address in Amsterdam. Enclose the card. Send the package today."

The man got an odd glint in his eye.

Barrabas put the pearls back onto the red-velvet display pad. "Make sure that these two pearls are the ones you send," the white-haired man said. "If I find out you've pulled a switch on me, my two friends here will drop by and chop your fingers off."

The shop owner looked past Barrabas to the pair of big men standing by the door—a black one in a sports shirt and shorts and a white one in a gray tank top and fatigue pants. The white man was a body builder and a clown.

"You'll have a hell of a time picking your nose," Nanos told him.

The black man did not smile. He had not changed his expression in the past ten minutes.

"I would never try to cheat a valued customer," the merchant said.

"Send them today," Barrabas said, pointing at the pearls on the pad.

Then the three men left the shop and continued down the winding street in the direction of the marina.

"Do you know how they used to collect pearls here?" Hayes asked. "They used slaves. They'd make the slaves load up the boats with rocks. Then, when they were out over the oyster beds, they'd tie a big rock around the neck of a slave and chuck him overboard. If he managed to untie the rock and come up with an oyster in his fist, they tied another rock around his neck and threw him over again. They had plenty of rocks."

"Must've had plenty of slaves, too," Nanos said.

"Yeah, unskilled labor. They didn't give 'em a swimming test before they put 'em to work," Hayes said. "No wonder black people aren't supposed to like the water."

"I guess that makes you the exception to the rule, huh?" Nanos said to the former U.S. Navy SEAL.

Hayes gave him a pained look. "No, man," he said, "the rule is racist bullshit. I'm no exception."

A small smile played over Barrabas's lips. The

rule was bullshit, all right, but Claude Hayes was definitely an exception. At the age of thirty-eight he had already lived many lives. He had left his middle-class family in Detroit to go to college in the South during the sixties. He had wanted to change things for his people. The progress had been slow and painful. And when Dr. Martin Luther King, Jr., was murdered in Memphis all the frustration and pent-up anger inside him exploded. The Deep South was a bad place to go on a rampage in 1968. He was sentenced to work on a chain gang. After two years' hard time he managed to escape. He changed his name to Claude Hayes and with forged papers joined the Navy. It was a good place to hide. But the price was high. Regimentation. He could not pay it. He was too independent, too guarded by his bitterness about his past. He went free lance to Africa, to Mozambique where he fought with FRELIMO to free his black brothers from Portuguese oppression. From then on, he drifted from one armed struggle to the next. Enclosed by the screams of battle, he became a quiet man, inside and out, living the only life that really suited him.

The warrior life.

The winding street ended in a broad, modern promenade that bordered a sparkling clean marina. In the slips were boats of all sizes and all kinds. What they had in common were gleaming white hulls, blue canvas and well-cared-for teak.

"That Bertram 32 would do us nice," Nanos said.

"This way," Hayes said, steering them to the left, away from the trawlers and sportfishers.

"Where are we going?" Nanos said. "The winners are all back thataway."

Hayes did not answer. And Nanos did not bother to repeat the question. He was content to wait and see. Hayes knew as much about boats as Nanos did and a hell of a lot more about this little corner of the world.

They walked to the very edge of the marina. A line of mangy scows was moored along the breakwater riprap. It looked like a floating scrap yard.

"Now, what the hell do you call that?" Nanos said, pointing to a wooden motor-sailer. It was about eighty feet long and of decidedly Middle Eastern design. Its main sail was trapezoidal in shape, with the longest side up. The only thing it had ever been painted with was bird crap.

"That's a dhow," Hayes said. He hailed the boat in Arabic, and a man stepped out on the foredeck. They exchanged a few more words and then the man waved. He climbed down a rope ladder to a dinghy, which he untied, and then began to row to shore.

"He's joking about us taking that thing," Nanos said to Barrabas. "It'll sink before it gets out of the breakwater."

"Now you're getting the picture," Hayes said.

Nanos just shook his head in disgust.

The skipper of the dhow was a little guy. He had on a dirty headdress, a sports coat he had been sleeping in for a couple of years and a pair of Gucci shoes without socks or laces. He had not shaved or bathed in a while. As he reached over the side to steady the dinghy against the breakwater, Barrabas caught a glimpse of a scarred and worn small-caliber automatic tucked into his belt.

They boarded the dinghy, and the skipper rowed the overloaded craft back to his boat. Hayes maintained a steady babble of conversation with the man. When they were all on the deck, Hayes turned to his friends and said, "This guy's name is Ahmad. He's interested in selling us his boat."

Nanos eyed the clutter and disrepair around them. "Yeah, I'll bet he is."

"He says it's one of the fastest on the entire coast."

"Fastest to the bottom, you mean."

Hayes frowned at the Greek. "Let's go have a look at the man's power plant," he said, gesturing for them to follow the skipper.

The area belowdecks was as untidy as what they had already seen. And much more fragrant. The little guy dragged aside a plywood sheet that covered the engine compartment.

"Chebbies," the skipper said proudly, showing them the black stubs of his teeth.

"Count 'em, Alex," Hayes said. "Four big blown Chevys."

"Holy shit!" Nanos exclaimed.

Barrabas was impressed, too. Not only by the number of 427s crammed into the small space, but by their absolutely spotless condition.

"The skipper, here, assures me," Hayes said, "that this tub will do better than forty knots. It was built to outrun the government patrol boats in the Gulf. He uses it to move blackmarket merchandise back and forth."

"And he's willing to sell it?" Barrabas asked.

"For the right price," Hayes answered. "He says he wants to retire."

"What does he want for it?"

Hayes and the skipper spoke a few more words. "He says he'll take thirty grand in cash, American."

"He'll *take*," Nanos grumbled. "For that much we could get a used Bertram."

"Yeah," Barrabas said, "we could ride in style as we get towed back to some shithole of an Iranian jail. Low profile is what we're after, even if we have to pay a high-profile price. Tell the guy okay, but with conditions. First, the boat has to be moved to the dock where Gunther has the battle gear stashed. You will drive the boat, Claude—before the sale. Check it out, make sure it's all he says it is. We'll pay him the full amount at dockside.''

Hayes explained the terms to the skipper. ''He'll go for it,'' the black man said.

They shook hands all around and then the boat owner rowed them back to shore. Hayes waited until the man was on his way back across the water, well out of earshot, then he said, ''The guy's a real slimeball, Colonel. We can't trust him. Arabs are hagglers by nature. He went for our proposition too fast. He's going to try and pull some crap on us. I know it.''

''What'll he do?'' Barrabas said. ''Turn us in to the police while we're loading the weapons?''

Hayes shook his head. ''Our skipper is a smuggler not an informer. He's a sharp bastard. He knows he'll get a lot more out of the deal if he steals the cargo and his boat back from us somewhere out in the Gulf.''

''How the fuck is he going to catch us?'' Nanos said. ''Do something to disable the engines?''

Hayes grinned. ''Those 'Chebbies' are his four sons. He wouldn't think of touching them. He'll probably have some people hidden in the boat. They'll wait until we're out at sea a ways, then jump us. After they kill us, they'll weigh us down and dump us.''

''We'd better arrange to leave port a bit early,'' Barrabas said. ''We're going to have to do a complete search after we clear the breakwater.''

''What're we going to do when we find them?'' Nanos said.

Barrabas shrugged. ''That's up to them.''

11

"What an armpit," Biondi said as he looked down on south-central Iran. It was not the first time he had made the observation that afternoon. For hours he and Gunther had been flying over the same type of terrain: dry, rocky, uninhabitable. A dead zone, broken only by occasional pockets of color, wheat fields and date orchards planted around an oasis.

Thirty minutes before, they had crossed the main north-south road and they were now following it toward Kerman. The sun was setting. In the distance ahead, the highway wound back and forth as it climbed bleak, purple mountains.

Gunther banked the Sikorsky to the right and cut his altitude to three hundred feet. Below them was the military base that was their destination.

"Are you okay?" Gunther asked.

"Yeah, sure," Biondi said.

"You don't look okay."

"I'm just a little wound up, that's all," Biondi told him. "Don't sweat it."

"Let me do all the talking down there."

"Fine with me."

Biondi stared out the window as Gunther swung the helicopter in for a landing. The airfield was a big one, built with U.S. technical and financial support. The planes sitting along the edge of the runway were American; the pilots who flew them and the mechanics who serviced them had been trained by Americans. It was all there to see, Biondi thought. The standard Third World dump job. We give in good faith; they shit on our heads.

But that was not what was really eating Biondi. He did not give a damn about wasted tax dollars or a bunch of twerps burning Uncle Sam in effigy. Biondi kept thinking about eight RH-53D Sea Stallion helicopters, about the brave men who had flown in them. They had come by night, too, from the south into this land of dirt and stones, on a mission to recover national honor. Eight choppers when the job called for twelve. Eight choppers equipped with inadequate dust filters. A mission doomed before it had begun.

There had been no recovery of honor on April 24, 1980; only sacrifice.

And tragic waste.

The more Biondi thought about it, the tighter the spring inside him twisted.

Gunther put the Sikorsky down on the tarmac, soft and easy. As they switched off the helicopter's engines a troop truck and two jeeps sped toward them from the hangar area. The jeeps stopped on one side, the truck on the other.

"Our hosts," Gunther said as he unstrapped himself from the seat.

A dozen men armed with automatic weapons jumped from the back of the truck and surrounded the Sikorsky.

"Yeah," Biondi said, "welcome to Iran."

He and Gunther exited the helicopter, hands raised high in the air. As the Dutchman started to walk toward the officers in the lead jeep, a big smile on his face, a soldier blocked his path with an M-16.

"Okay, okay," Gunther said, retreating as the man jabbed him in the stomach with the muzzle of the automatic rifle.

They were forced to turn and lean against the Sikorsky while the soldiers slapped them down for concealed weapons. Then they were escorted to the jeep.

If Gunther was fazed by the rough treatment, he did not show it. He extended his hand to the ranking officer. "You must be Colonel Shaigān," he said.

The colonel, a stout man with a close-cropped gray beard, ignored the offered hand. He barked a curt order in Pharsee. The soldiers started unloading the chopper. The first gearbox went into the lead jeep.

"Be our guest, Colonel," Gunther said.

Then the prodding with the M-16 resumed.

Gunther and Biondi were herded into the second jeep and driven at gunpoint across the airfield to a row of Quonset huts beside the main hangars.

"You're real tight with these guys, aren't you?" Biondi said as they were pulled out of the jeep.

"It's a game they're playing," Gunther told him. "Just string along."

The two men were marched into the colonel's office. The tail-rotor gearbox was deposited on the colonel's desk. Gunther and Biondi were made to stand in front of it. After Colonel Shaigān sat down, he gestured at a man in mechanic's coveralls who stood in the doorway. The guy hurried to the desk with his toolbox. He took out a magnifying glass and began examining the outside of the gearbox, checking part numbers, seals and inspection stamps.

When he finished, the mechanic addressed the colonel in Pharsee. Colonel Shaigān nodded.

Biondi saw Gunther's smile widen as the mechanic began attacking the gearbox seals. He was going to take the cover off and have a look at the innards.

"You realize, of course, Colonel," the Dutchman said, "that you'll never be able to properly seal that box again. You're destroying a fifty-thousand-dollar replacement part for nothing."

The colonel didn't answer.

It was truth time.

When the cover came off, Biondi expected to

see a box filled with nothing but scrap metal packed in heavy grease. But what was in the grease did not look like scrap metal. To the mechanic it looked like what it was supposed to be. He gave it a clean bill of health.

"Now that you've satisfied yourself," Gunther said, "we'd like to collect the second half of the payment due and clear out."

"Do you know what the penalty is for smuggling in this country?" Colonel Shaigān said.

"Here it comes," Biondi muttered.

"You said something?" Shaigān demanded.

"Yeah, a colorful expression from the land of my forefathers. *Va fan cullo*."

"Meaning?"

"Let a smile be your umbrella."

Gunther flashed Biondi a warning with his eyes. Then he said, "Colonel, this particular smuggling job was done at the express request of your government."

"Regrettable. Yet, sometimes we are forced to deal with criminal elements from the West. We always deal on our own terms."

"The terms were already agreed upon."

Colonel Shaigān shook his head. "You tried to take advantage of us, of our need for spare parts. You doubled the going price for the gearboxes. That, too, is a crime in this country."

"Nobody would sell you the parts, at any price," Gunther said. "In my country a deal is a deal and a man sticks to his word."

Shaigan laughed. He rose from his chair and leaned over the desk toward them. "Your Western concept of honor among thieves. Typical of the way you glorify the worst elements in an already corrupt society. You see, we have no rules of conduct when it comes to bargaining with criminals. And as for thieves, we cut off their hands."

Biondi was only a yard from the man, and he could feel his self-control slipping. The Iranian colonel was so smug, so confidently superior. He was the cheat who brags after he wins. He belonged to a nation controlled by cheats, blowhards, frauds. An image popped into Biondi's head. Bodies rolled in clear plastic, unwrapped for the TV cameras in Tehran, exhibited like trophies.

Unearned trophies.

That was the part that hacked at Biondi's guts.

The colonel unsnapped the flap of his holster and slid out a Government Colt .45. "It only takes two Pasdaran witnesses to legally condemn a criminal to death. We are also empowered to carry out the death sentence." He cocked back the Colt's hammer with his thumb and pointed the pistol at them. "I could kill you both here and now."

Biondi did not think.

He moved.

In a blur he grabbed the pistol from the top, jamming his thumb between the hammer and the firing pin. Before the man could counter, Biondi wrenched the weapon from his grasp. He rammed the muzzle under Colonel Shaigān's nose and held it there.

"Blink once and you're gone," Biondi said.

For long seconds no one in the room moved.

Gunther broke the nerve-racking silence. "Hey, come on, Vince, it's only money," he said as he stepped around the desk. "We don't want a whole lot of trouble over a few dollars. We want to keep doing business with these nice people. Develop a good working relationship."

The Dutchman slowly, carefully slipped his hand over the gun.

Biondi let him take it.

"I'm really sorry about that," Gunther said as he returned the weapon butt-first to the officer. "My friend, here, has a very short fuse. We gladly accept your new terms. Consider the Cobra parts completely paid for. Now, if you will refuel us, we'll be on our way."

The colonel reholstered his handgun and pulled himself together. There was a loss of face involved only if he admitted to being scared out of his wits. He could afford to be magnanimous. After all, he had just ripped off the Western cowards for more than two million dollars.

On the way back to the Sikorsky, Gunther said, "You crazy bastard, you almost wrecked everything."

Biondi gave him a cold look.

"Do you know how lucky we were back there?"

"Yeah, I know," Biondi said. "He could have blinked."

12

The dhow's four Chevys rumbled as Hayes steered the boat past moored white yachts and headed out of the marina.

Barrabas looked back at the fairy lights of the promenade. He knew that in some waterfront café the former owner of the dhow would be watching their departure and rubbing his grubby palms together. The man did not know what sort of cargo the Americans were moving, but he knew it would have to be of great value for them to have spent thirty thousand dollars on a boat to carry it.

"What do you think, Colonel?" O'Toole said.

"I think everyone stays on deck until we get ready to make our search. I don't want anyone hurt at this stage. We can't afford to lose any personnel."

"Should I go ahead and pass out small arms?"

"Yeah, pistols and knives," he said. "And remind them all that if they've got to shoot to check behind their target first. If they can, they should aim toward the outside of the boat. The bulkheads on this tub wouldn't stop spit."

O'Toole used a crowbar to pry the lid off a small, sturdily built wooden crate and started passing out guns and holsters. Each of the mercenaries had provided his or her own handgun. Though they were different makes, Walther, Browning, Beretta, among others, all were chambered for a 9mm round, a cartridge available in virtually every country in the world. Lee's choice was the Heckler and Koch P-7, light, compact, easily controlled. Billy Two's stainless-steel S&W auto was the flashiest weapon of the bunch.

In the weak light of a single bulb strung from the main mast, the SOBs shrugged into military shoulder holsters and checked pistol magazines. The night was dead calm, oppressively hot and muggy even on the water.

Barrabas buckled on a black web belt that supported a holstered Browning Hi-Power automatic on his left hip. The 14-shot weapon's butt jutted forward, cross rigged for a right-hand draw. On his right hip a stiletto dangled in its slim stiff sheath.

"Goose it some, Claude," he said as they cleared the breakwater.

Hayes used both hands to ease the four throttle levers forward. The dhow surged eagerly ahead, the ropes dangling from its furled sail slapping the mast, its bow hissing as it sliced through the still sea.

The movement of air was welcome.

Barrabas moved from the helm near the stern of the boat to the mast amidships. He waved for his mercenaries to gather around.

"You know what we've got to do before we get on with business," he said. "I know you're all pumped up. You want to get in on it. The trouble is, the space belowdecks is too cramped. If we all go down there we're only going to get in one another's way. We'll make it easier for whoever's hiding to do us some damage. This is a job for four. Four of the smallest. They'll have the most room to maneuver."

O'Toole grinned. "That means me, Lee, Chen and Beck."

"Right," Barrabas said. "Lee and Chen start at the bow. You and Beck work toward them from the stern. Don't overlook anything. These guys could be hiding in the woodwork."

"More likely the bilges," Nanos said.

"Come on, Chen, it's hide-and-seek time," the black-haired woman said as she drew the H&K automatic from shoulder leather under her left armpit. She had cut the sleeves off her black T-shirt to give herself more freedom of movement. The shirt now stuck to the middle of her back, soaked through with perspiration.

She climbed down the steep stairs, following the Chinese American. At the bottom they stood back to back and surveyed the dimly lit hold. It was not large, but it was full of clutter: wooden boxes, piles of rope.

"They could be anywhere," Chen said. "We're going to have to turn all this junk upside down."

"What's behind that door?" Lee asked, indicating a closed, windowless entryway on the bow side of the companionway.

"Forward cabin or storage locker," Chen replied.

"I'll check it out," Lee offered. "You start in here."

She tried the doorknob with her left hand. It turned. Her grip on the H&K P-7 tightened, engaging the weapon's squeeze cocking system. It was ready to rip. She pushed the door open half a foot then slipped her hand inside. Her fingers found the light switch. When she flicked it nothing happened.

"Figures," she muttered, taking a flashlight from the rear pocket of her fatigues. She turned on her light, then kicked the door open, dropping to a squat, the H&K and the flashlight thrust out in front of her.

It was a sail locker.

Six feet wide at the doorway wall, half that at the far wall, with five feet in between. It was as neat as the rest of the boat. Along the right side there were long shelves filled with folded and stacked sail, but there was much more cloth on the floor, piled in great rumpled heaps.

Lee shined the light in the crack between door

and jamb, making sure there was no one behind it. Then she slipped into the small room.

It smelled musty.

And it was suffocatingly hot.

The three shelves on her right were easily long enough to conceal a man. But with the sail stacked on them it was impossible to tell if they were deep enough.

The sailcloth heaps on the floor were her first order of business. She kicked and jumped on the piles.

Nothing.

Her feet only raised dust.

It had to be the shelves, then.

She stuck the flashlight's barrel in her mouth, freeing both hands. With her left she jerked a stack of sail from the bottom shelf while she held the P-7 rock-steady in her right. There was no one behind the stacks, but there was plenty of room back there.

As she reached for a stack on the second shelf something rustled behind her. Even as she started to turn she knew it was too late; she had blown it. The edge of a hand hit the base of her neck, and her knees buckled.

The flashlight fell.

The room went dark.

Lee did not black out for more than a split second. Even so, when she came to, she could not control her limbs. There was no strength in her fingers. Something scrambled from the second shelf, then the H&K automatic was ripped from her hand.

Before she could recover completely she was seized from behind. A dirty hand clamped over her mouth, and the cold snout of a pistol was jammed behind her right ear.

She felt a hard, sweaty body against her back.

Definitely a man's body.

And he felt hers. Sweaty, yes. Hard, no.

The hand slipped from her mouth, down over her chest, molding itself to the firm contours there. She did not struggle.

A groan of surprise came from over her shoulder, then a few hoarse words she did not understand.

The locker door swung shut. And the light came on. When it did, Lee saw a man pulling his hand back from the bare bulb. It had been partially unscrewed. He was in his early twenties, dressed in a pair of cutoff jeans wet with sweat. His longish brown hair hung down in dripping plaits. His pupils were the size of flyspecks.

Whacked out of his skull, Lee thought. And his buddy, too, no doubt. They'd have to be to take on a job like this. Hiding for hours in the terrible heat, waiting for the chance to murder strangers.

She could not see the man who was holding her. He was bigger than the one in front of her, though. The man in front tucked her captured

H&K into the waistband of his shorts, then held a grimy finger to his lips and shook his head.

They wanted her to keep quiet.

To underscore the point, the man behind her twisted the muzzle of the pistol against her flesh.

Murder was not what was currently on their minds.

The guy in front approached her from the side, avoiding the possibility of getting kneed. He tugged the T-shirt out of the waistband of her fatigues and slipped his hand up under it. His pal, meanwhile, turned his attention to the front zipper of the fatigues.

Their fingers felt like spiders. Sticky spiders.

She let her arms drop to her sides as if giving in to the whole deal. She could feel the guy with the gun getting all worked up. He was real dumb. He could not control her head with his hand in her pants. And if he could not control her head, he had nothing.

Dr. Hatton had spent a lot of years learning how to put people back together; she had spent even longer learning how to take them apart.

She shifted to the side, as if trying to evade the touch of the man in front of her. Actually, she could hardly feel what he was doing through the heavy-duty cups and wires of the bra she wore into combat. What she was doing was clearing the path to her primary target. With the gun at her head, she had one chance. She had to deliver a killing blow on the first try. She had started failed hearts with a single punch of her hand. The same blow dealt to a healthy pump could stop it cold.

Or so the theory went.

She leaned her backside into the man with the gun, pushing him firmly against the wall. The heavy breathing, the pawing was making her sick. It was time to end it. One way or another.

Lee extended her right arm to its limit and made a fist. Then she snapped her arm back with blinding speed, twisting her torso to increase power. She buried the point of her elbow under the man's sternum. With his back pressed flat against the wall, there was nowhere for the force to go, except in.

Something crunched under her elbow. Something gurgled over her shoulder. Then the pistol's muzzle came away from her ear.

Even as she drove her right arm into him, she was reaching out with her left. Her hand closed on the grip of her H&K, which was sticking out of the waistband of the man in front of her.

She pulled the trigger.

In the confined space the reports were deafening.

So were the screams.

Lee fired five times before the man crumpled. Then she turned. The other guy was in fibrillation, eyes rolled up, tongue protruding, limbs quivering. She put a single bullet through his face.

Another gunshot boomed in answer from the other side of the locker door. The slug tore through the wall a foot from her head, slamming into and through the far wall.

Three shots followed so close together they sounded like full-auto. Lee opened the door a crack and peered around the bottom edge.

Chen was standing in the middle of the small hold with his back to her. The Beretta 92-S in his raised right hand spat 9mm slugs as a figure popped up from behind a crate, gun in fist. Wood and bone splintered under the hail of bullets. Lee could hear the difference between the hits. Hit meat thwacked.

Then Chen stopped shooting. As he walked over to look behind the crate, she stood up, straightened her clothes and moved forward.

There was another pirate on his back on the floor. One of his arms was flung out, hand extended as if trying to reach the grip of the revolver he had dropped.

He was never going to make it. His mouth was a gory pit, dug by a trio of 9mm Silvertips.

"Is he dead?" Lee asked as Chen turned toward her.

"And then some. You okay?"

"Yeah, come and look in here." She showed him the carnage in the sail locker. Together they discovered the sliding panel and compartment where the men who attacked her had hidden.

"When you cut loose in here," Chen said,

"those other barf bags thought it was the signal to open up."

O'Toole and Beck peered into the locker over Chen's shoulder.

"You guys are a little late," Chen said.

"Yeah," O'Toole said. "Looks like the show's over."

"We didn't find anything in the stern," Beck told them.

"This is probably the lot," the Irishman said. "If there were more they would have showed when the shooting started. We'll go over it all one more time, just to be sure."

BARRABAS WATCHED as Nanos and Boone slid the last of the corpses over the stern, into the glistening white froth of the dhow's wake.

"Those guys will never turn up on any beach. I guarantee it," Hayes said. "The sharks in these waters are big and hungry."

"Time to kill the running lights and see what this boat can really do," Barrabas said.

The black man smiled. He shut off all the lights above deck except for the tiny one that illuminated the compass. He shoved the throttle levers forward and the quartet of 427s bellowed.

"Christ!" Nanos groaned, clutching at the stern rail as the sudden surge nearly toppled him overboard.

The boat's bow rose higher and higher as it quickly accelerated. Its wake was no longer a sedate bubbling; it was a churning torrent of foam.

At planing speed the debris that littered the deck started to fly, to roll, to creep toward the stern. To avoid being hit or buried, Barrabas and the others moved to the bow and put their backs to the warm wind.

The voyage was not a smooth one, even though the sea was flat. At the rate they were traveling every surface ripple became a whitecap, jarring craft and passengers. Overhead, in a moonless sky, the stars bounced wildly at each rhythmic impact.

They rode in silence for an hour and a half until they could make out an irregular line on the horizon ahead—a band of impenetrable darkness that blocked out the stars.

It was Iran.

Barrabas walked back to the stern and told Hayes to cut speed. As he throttled back, the boat's bow glided down from planing height and the maddening vibration stopped.

"Billy," Barrabas said, "get up in the bow. Boone take the stern. Watch for patrol boats. Liam, let's get ready for the landing."

Even though the shore was eight miles away, there was no point in waiting any longer. If Iranian patrols caught them, there would be no talking their way out of it. The guns and other gear would be found. To the Iranians that could only mean one thing: mercs who meant their country no good. If the SOBs could not outrun Iranian pursuit, if they were caught, they would have to fight.

And the mission would be flushed.

O'Toole and Nanos began prying open the long wooden crates the team had loaded on the foredeck in Bahrain.

"Special today on Kevlar undies. One per customer," Nanos said, holding up a wrap-around chest and back protector. He passed out the body armor to everyone. In the dim starlight the SOBs stripped to the waist and strapped on the vests. Lee stripped, too, without a second thought. She was among brothers.

The squad members pulled camouflage shirts on over the armor, then picked up packs and lined up in front of O'Toole.

He had uncrated the weapons and ammo. There were M-79 grenade launchers with HE and CS gas projectiles. Silencer-equipped Colt XM-177s and Uzis. And four M-21 sniper rifles. Each merc was issued two weapons, depending on assignment, and given ammunition and hand grenades.

Other than Lee's medical kit and water canteens, no desert survival supplies were given out. The omission underscored what the Soldiers of Barrabas already knew. If something went wrong, if they did not get into the site or get away on schedule, nothing they could carry on their backs was going to be of any help.

Gradually the band of darkness dead ahead blocked out more and more of the night sky. Then they glided into the solid wall of heat thrown off by the Iranian land mass. In an instant the air temperature jumped ten degrees. They were well inside the range of shore batteries. The sound of wavelets lapping on sand could be heard over the soft rumble of the engines. Then they saw the vague outline of a cove.

"This is it," Hayes said softly. "Can't take her in any closer because of the low tide. I know it looks like a long way to the beach, but trust me; the water a hundred yards in is only waist deep."

"Drop the hook," Barrabas said.

At this stage of the game there was no wiseassing. Until they got in the helicopter and off the beach, they were vulnerable as hell. With the boat anchored in seventy-five feet of water, they inflated the ten-man life raft they had brought along. In five minutes the SOBs were in the warm shallows, working their way up onto the broad stretch of sand.

"Signal," Barrabas told O'Toole.

The Irishman took out a flashlight and blinked it five times.

An answering light winked atop a ridge of dunes due east. Two long, three short.

"That's them," O'Toole said.

"Okay, Claude," the colonel said, "do your number on the boat."

Hayes slipped back to the water. He pushed the raft as far as he could, then scrambled in and rowed back to the dhow. After tying the raft securely to the stern, he climbed aboard, went belowdecks and opened the seacocks. The dhow was already beginning to list to port as Hayes knifed into the water in a shallow dive. By the time he reached the beach again, the boat was bottom up and sinking fast.

Only O'Toole waited on the sand. He helped Hayes don pack and weapons, then picked up his own M-21 and moved east at a fast trot.

Hayes followed, the water trapped inside his canvas desert boots squishing at every step.

13

The forklift emerged from the bunker doorway into the blinding glare of the compound's floodlights. The machine strained as it climbed the ramp to ground level. Laid across its twin prongs was a long, heavy wooden crate. Standing atop the crate was Mohamadi Razod.

A hundred Pasdars followed behind the forklift, thrusting their assault rifles in the air as they chanted his name. "Ra-zod! Ra-zod! Ra-zod!"

The demonstration was spontaneous. A display of respect and admiration, of sheer fundamentalist zeal. It was an ecstatic moment for the captain. There was no doubt in his mind nor in the minds of his guardsmen who was really responsible for the successful completion of the nuclear project. The scientists were mere tinkers, educated lackeys. A less inspired man would not have had the courage to drive them way beyond their limits, to squeeze them until blood seeped from their eyes like tears.

All for the glory of the Government of God.

Razod was certain his superiors in Tehran would recognize the selflessness of his accomplishment and reward him accordingly. A new command. A promotion. He would be a national hero, cheered not by hundreds but by hundreds of thousands.

"Ra-zod! Ra-zod!" Their chanting would shake buildings, rattle windows.

Basking in adoration, both present and anticipated, the captain rode the atomic weapon all the way to the truck. He hopped down to direct the loading. At his signal three men unlocked the tailgate and lowered it. Once the forklift had raised the crate to the proper height, a dozen more Pasdars climbed up into the truck and gently eased the device off the prongs, onto the bed, under its camouflage canvas cover.

The truck's springs groaned from the load.

"Slide it farther forward," Razod told them. "It will ride better up there."

They pushed the crate to within a foot of the cab of the truck.

"Fine. That will do fine," Razod said. "Shut the tailgate." He gestured to the two noncoms in charge of the convoy's twenty-four-man guard force.

At once they ordered the heavily armed Pasdars into the backs of two other trucks. The drivers of all three trucks and the lead vehicle, a jeep, started their engines. They revved with gusto, sending plumes of whitish smoke drifting across the compound.

They were eager to be off, but they could wait.

"Hamid!" the captain shouted. He waved impatiently at the rear of the crowd where the men in white stood.

Dr. Hamid meekly approached.

"Well?" Razod demanded.

"I am sorry, Captain, we will need another few minutes. There have been some further difficulties. . . ."

"I don't want to hear any more of your miserable excuses. If you think my leaving camp will make things easier for you, you are mistaken. Lieutenant Yazdi is going to see to it that you finish before any of you sleep again. Do you understand, Hamid?"

The scientist nodded.

There was laughter from the ranks.

Razod smiled at Hamid. "If you only have a few more minutes' work, as you claim, you will get your well-deserved rest tonight."

The captain stepped over to the passenger side of the middle truck, the one loaded with the bomb, and got in.

The Pasdars left behind sent up a rousing cheer as the convoy rolled out through the camp's main gate in a cloud of dust.

Razod settled back into his seat. The ride to the paved highway was going to be long, slow and uncomfortable. In the truck's headlights he could just make out the rear of the troop carrier twenty feet ahead. It was obscured by swirling clouds of dust. At least he was not in the last truck. He took a red handkerchief from his pants pocket and tied it over his nose and mouth to block the dust.

As they rounded a turn, a gust of wind blew the fine powder off to the left. In the beams of the headlights the road was dead white, the rocks that lined it bleached of all color. Beyond the perimeter of the lights, darkness was absolute; it was as if they were traveling in a tunnel.

Razod wanted to get some sleep, but the road would not cooperate. The potholes and the washboard sections were too close together to permit even a catnap.

Razod turned his attention to the truck's dashboard. The picture pasted there was dimly visible in the light of the instrument panel. The captain filled in the details from memory—the deep-set, burning eyes under wild and lengthy black eyebrows.

It was the picture of the man in the beard.

That same likeness was spread over the entire camp in all sizes, all forms. It was on T-shirts, on buttons, on decals stuck to the stocks of assault rifles. The fierce and holy visage looked down and sanctified everything, reminding those who served that God was with them, that they were doing His will.

As the truck jounced and bumped along, the captain drifted off into a waking dream. He imagined himself already a general at the head of a vast army. An army poised to strike against the principal enemy, Amrika—America. At his command, wave after wave of Pasdaran troops assault the enemy position, soaking up bullets and shrapnel like human sponges. Even as his men fall, he commits more to the cause. And still more. They do not hesitate, do not question his divine leadership. They charge on, only to be ground to pulp by enemy fire. But, inevitably, the hated enemy is worn down, exhausted, out of ammunition, and succumbs to the righteous fury of God's army. Razod personally leads the television crews through a scene of unimaginable carnage, his uniform spotless, perfectly creased, his boots gleaming like black mirrors.

It was amazing and wonderful how his desires and God's will seemed to coincide.

Razod's reverie burst as the driver slammed on the brakes and cut the wheel hard to the left.

"What!" the captain cried, his heart thudding sickeningly as they swerved and skidded around the rear of the truck stopped directly in front of them. From behind there came a terrible squeal of brakes. Razod braced himself for a collision with the following vehicle.

None came.

He jumped down from the cab, livid with anger. Men were already piling out of the first truck.

"It's the tire, sir," the driver said.

Razod walked around the bumper. Sure enough, the right front tire was flat.

"Fix it!" he snarled.

As his men scurried to find tools and a spare, Razod looked at his convoy, ringed in the glow of headlights. Overhead there was nothing between them and the stars. For miles and miles in every direction there was no cover. A chill crept up his spine.

"Cut all lights!" he ordered.

"But, sir, we have to see in order to repair the...."

"Pray for guidance, Corporal."

DR. HAMID LEANED BACK against the edge of his desk. All around him the other scientists were hugging and congratulating one another. It was the first time in more than a month that there had been laughter in the rad lab. The fourth bomb stood in the middle of the room, the lid section of its cylindrical case ready to be bolted shut.

The only person in the room not smiling was Lieutenant Yazdi. He watched the proceedings with arms folded across his chest, unimpressed by their accomplishment.

In a way, Dr. Hamid wished that the captain had remained so he could have witnessed the little scene. Not that Razod would have appreciated it, either. Undoubtedly, he would have mentioned all the delays. It was better that he was not there. He would have found a way to spoil their happiness.

Lieutenant Yazdi cleared his throat and in a loud voice announced, "You will all come with me." He gestured toward the door.

Dr. Hamid quieted his fellow researchers.

"Captain Razod," Yazdi continued, "wants to show his gratitude for all you have done. He has had a special meal prepared for you in the mess hall. Please, come with me."

It was an offer the scientists did not dare refuse. They could not turn down an honor from the camp commander without risking his wrath. And besides, all of them, Hamid included, were too elated and too exhausted to quibble.

Outside the door to the rad lab, four armed Pasdars waited. They swung into step behind the scientists.

Yazdi smiled reassuringly at Hamid. And they continued down the zigzag hallway. The lieutenant marveled at how stupid the educated could be, how ready they were to believe what suited them.

At the entrance to the dormitory, another four Pasdars joined the rear guard. As they neared the mess-hall door, Yazdi moved to the head of the group. He blocked the doorway with upraised arms.

"Before you enjoy yourselves," he said, "there is one more little thing the captain wants you to do."

There were groans of disbelief.

"Outside."

Dr. Hamid tried to placate the officer. "Whatever it is, lieutenant, surely it can wait until tomorrow, after we've had some rest."

"No. It cannot wait."

The Pasdars used the butts of their assault rifles to drive the scientists out the bunker door and up the ramp into the compound.

"What do you think you're doing?" Hamid demanded. "You can't treat us this way!"

Hamid's protests fell on deaf ears.

The scientists were herded over to a toolshed.

"Each of you take a shovel," Yazdi ordered.

The twelve-man research team looked to its senior member for guidance. Dr. Hamid waved his hands, urging calm. Evidently, Razod was not through with them. He required some further degradation, more penance for their academic triumphs, for the corrupt values they had presumably absorbed during years in the West. It was true to form.

"All right, all right," Hamid said resignedly. "Whatever it is you want us to do, we will do. If it's latrines you want dug, we will dig them."

"I'm glad you are all being so sensible," Yazdi replied.

He meant it, too. If the scientists had decided to stand their ground in the bunker, it would have made for a very messy situation. The lieutenant would have been forced to execute them on the spot. Then Pasdars would have had to lug the corpses out and dig a common grave.

The scientists were joking and laughing again as they shouldered the shovels. The lieutenant marched them out the front gates. Three gates. One for each perimeter fence.

"Pick it up, let's move," he snapped, clapping his hands at the ragged line of men.

The exhausted scientists complied, with encouragement from the Islamic Revolutionary Guards, who kicked and prodded them along.

As they trotted down the dirt road, Dr. Hamid kept telling himself that as long as they did not give the Pasdars an excuse for violence, as long as they took their punishment, everything was going to be all right.

"To your right!" Yazdi shouted. "Off the road!"

As the column turned, Dr. Hamid looked back at the lights of the compound and felt a terrible sinking sensation in the pit of his stomach. They were a half mile away. Too far for latrines. Then he was forced to put all his attention on the ground underfoot. There were little rocks and big rocks and they were all loose. There was no question of picking one's way around the more treacherous spots; the Pasdars would not allow it. They kept bashing the butts of their rifles into the stragglers' backs.

Hamid's breath came in erratic gasps. His legs were weak from the headlong run down the road. He tried desperately to keep up with the younger men, but the larger boulders were hurdles he could barely clear. His foot caught on one and he went down hard on his face, taking two other scientists with him. The tangle of limbs and shovels tripped up those who came behind.

"Get up!" Yazdi shouted, kicking viciously at legs and buttocks. "Get up and run!"

A short burst of automatic-rifle fire ripped over their heads. The scientists scrambled to their feet, grabbed shovels and ran.

Dr. Hamid's lower face was wet. So was his chin and throat. There was blood pouring from his nose. He had to breathe through his mouth to keep from choking on the blood. But he ran, too. Blind panic drove him on, forcing him to lift legs of lead. They were heading farther and farther away from the halo of light from the compound.

They followed a gravel wash that made the going easier, and their descent into darkness even more rapid. The wash ended in a five-foot-high ridge of eroded rock.

Yazdi and the Pasdars drove them over it.

Some of the men were sobbing as they climbed down onto fine, white sand. It was an ancient streambed. Soft, easy to turn. There was no longer any doubt in their minds what they had been brought out to do.

The lieutenant pushed them into a line with their backs to the ridge. "I want a pit," he said. "Start digging. I'll tell you when to stop."

"No!" Hamid said. "Don't dig."

The scientists held their shovels still.

"On whose orders are you doing this?" Hamid demanded. "By what authority?"

Bluff was the only weapon left to Hamid.

Yazdi unholstered his side arm.

Dr. Hamid took that as the answer to his question. "Then you have no authority," he said, his voice rising in pitch. "If you think the government will let something like this pass, you are making a terrible mistake. We have done something important for our country. We are heroes."

The lieutenant cracked the Beretta M-1951's slide back and then let it snap forward, cocking the hammer and jacking a live 9mm round under the firing pin. He aimed the pistol at Hamid's heart.

"Then dig like heroes," he said.

All of the scientists set to work. Each man's shovel seemed to weigh a hundred pounds; hands were clumsy, numbed. Some of the men cried as they dug, others muttered prayers. Dr. Hamid remembered al-Barani's prediction about what would happen once their usefulness to the regime was over. In desperation he spoke up again.

"Lieutenant, don't do this. Don't waste us. We can do other things; we can do hard labor, anything."

Yazdi gestured with the Beretta for Hamid to keep digging.

A painful lump rose in Hamid's throat. The end of his life was before him, a gradually deepening black pit.

One of the scientists let out an animal howl and broke ranks, throwing down his shovel and running like a madman through the line of Pasdars. As he dashed out onto the wide fan of sand, a second researcher dropped his shovel and raced after him.

The Islamic Revolutionary Guards did not start shooting at once. They let their targets run for thirty yards, and even then they did not shoot directly at the fleeing men. They shot at their heels, making the scientists cut back and forth frantically, making them shriek in terror. When the escapees were sixty yards away, the Pasdars opened up in earnest. The muzzles of their assault rifles belched blue flame and heavy slugs sliced the still air, crisscrossing at the intended points of impact, chopping the scientists down. They flopped to the sand and stayed there.

Yazdi grabbed two of the scientists by the shoulder and shoved them in the direction of their dead comrades. "Go on, bring them back. Hurry up."

As the men walked away, the Pasdars took aim at the backs of their heads.

Hamid's mind was a whirl with wild, crazy thoughts. If they all broke free, in the confusion perhaps some would escape. Some, but not him. He was too slow. Too old. He watched as the researchers returned, dragging the corpses by the feet.

"What have we done to deserve this!" he wailed.

"Keep digging," the lieutenant said.

When the thirty-foot-long pit was two yards deep and two yards wide, Yazdi ordered them to stop. With his foot he rolled the two corpses into the open grave. "All of you," he said, "get down in there with them."

The scientists dropped their shovels and slipped into the pit. Some looked up at the stars; some could only stare down at the sand.

"On your knees!"

Dr. Hamid blubbered and wept as he dropped down. His hands clutched at the dry sand. It was the last thing he would feel. The acrid stink of fear in the pit was the last thing he would smell.

On Yazdi's command, the Pasdars walked to the right end of the trench. Each stood before one of the kneeling scientists. Eight rifle bolts clacked, then weapons were aimed at the first eight men.

"Fire!" Yazdi said.

Hamid was not lucky enough to be in the first round.

He was number nine.

Assault rifles barked, and bodies were hurled back against the rear of the pit. When they bounced forward, they were as limp as rag dolls.

A warm and heavy weight pressed against Hamid's side.

It was trembling violently.

He wanted to scream, but he could not draw air. He wanted to jump and run, even though he knew it was futile, but his legs were numb, his own body shaking.

The Pasdars walked along the edge of the pit above him. They took aim at the second group of kneeling men.

Hamid tried to think of a prayer, but his mind was reeling. Though he was looking down at his thighs, he was aware of the gun sight, the gun bore trained on him. He could feel the intended track of the bullet running straight through his head.

Then his turn came.

The lieutenant shouted.

Assault rifles cracked.

Yazdi watched the three men in white coats re-coil in the light of muzzle-flashes, their skulls shattered. Like soft dominoes they slumped over on their sides in the ditch.

"Make sure," he said.

It was not a coup de grace.

It was a melee.

The Pasdars fired into the pit, their weapons on full automatic.

The lieutenant laughed. In the flickering strobe of gunfire, under the hail of bullets, the bodies jerked and gesticulated wildly. It was a grisly takeoff on silent films. A comedy of splat-tering gore.

"Enough!" he said. He gestured to four of the

Pasdars. "Cover the bodies. And don't forget to bring back all the shovels. The rest of you, come with me."

Yazdi headed back for the camp compound, a smile on his lips.

Mohamadi Razod would have been satisfied.

IN DARKNESS two men struggled to pull the truck wheel from its lug bolts. They grunted and strained at the task.

"Shh!" Captain Razod hissed. "Quiet!"

Off in the distance he heard the faint sounds of popping and crackling.

It was rifle fire.

"What is it, sir?" one of the Pasdars asked.

"Our scholars must have completed the fourth bomb," Razod said. "They're being rewarded."

In the distance there was more crackling.

Scattered chuckles came from the soldiers leaning against the truck.

"If you don't hurry up and change that tire," the captain said, "some of you will get the same reward."

The Pasdars returned to work. They got the flat tire and wheel off. It was even more difficult to seat the replacement wheel on the lugs. Fingers and knuckles were scraped and bruised.

Razod listened to them groaning in the dark. He was irritated. Given the distance the convoy had covered, he might as well have waited for the scientists to finish. He could have commanded the execution squad himself. They would have to make up the lost time on the main highway.

As they were jacking down the truck the Pasdars standing next to the captain said, "I hear something. What's that noise?"

Again Razod silenced the crew.

It was a droning sound. Too far away to tell whether it was coming or going, but the captain recognized it at once.

"It's nothing," he assured them. "Just a helicopter."

14

The Sikorsky flew without navigation lights, a shadow racing north across the night sky. The only illumination inside the craft was the feeble glow from the instrument panel. It bathed Gunther Dykstra's face in ghastly green. As they closed on the target, he banked the helicopter wide to the east, giving everyone a good long look.

Barrabas swore at what he saw.

The compound was lit up like a used-car lot. The halo of light extended out onto the plain for more than three hundred yards. It extended a similar distance up the saddle and south facing sides of the twin peaks. A red aircraft-warning beacon flashed on and off atop the tower on the easternmost peak.

Concealment had not been a concern of the installation's designers, and the colonel knew why. All of the above-ground emplacements, the guard towers, the listening posts, the triple fences, were not meant to hold off a determined opposition force. They were meant to give early warning, to stall an attack long enough for a retreat into the bunker complex where personnel and equipment would be safe until aid from a nearby military base could be summoned.

From an altitude of five thousand feet the landscape beyond the two mountains, to the north and west, looked like a solid wall of purple black. Beyond the peaks was a labyrinth of low hills and narrow, twisting valleys rising to even higher mountains on the horizon.

Gunther turned due north again, taking the Sikorsky down as he did so. They crossed the dirt road at a distance of three miles from the camp gates. Gunther quickly cut the altitude even further, down to one hundred fifty feet. They swept headlong toward the wall of purple black. As they neared it, it became less solid looking. The dim outlines of slopes, ridges and canyons appeared.

"Hang on back there," Gunther said as he cut back the air speed. He swung the Sikorsky around a steep hillside and down a winding valley.

Out the open side door, the rugged terrain was a blur. Barrabas turned to look at his crew. Eyeballs and teeth glowed out of faces smeared with nonreflective camouflage makeup. It was *some* minstrel show. A familiar tension squeezed at his guts. The last-doubt syndrome. He knew every commander worth his salt felt it at such a moment. Had he drawn the right conclusions, made the right choices? Would this attack plan hold up under the weight of countless unknowns? Had he given his people the best odds of surviving?

The Sikorsky suddenly climbed fifty feet to clear a rounded hilltop, then dropped back down into the darkness of a wider canyon.

"This is it, Colonel," Biondi said from the copilot's seat. "Landing zone number one."

"Take us down."

Dust billowed as they descended, obliterating their view of the dim canyon floor. When they were still five feet up, Barrabas jumped. He felt the ground's-jarring impact all the way to his hips. The tension in his belly vanished at once. There was no longer any room for doubts.

Hayes and Billy Two hit the ground seconds after him. The three men crouched as the Sikorsky lifted off and sped west.

Before the dust settled, Barrabas was up and moving at a slow jog. Hayes and Billy Two followed, single file. All their gear was battened down, rattleproof in their packs. And their weapons were securely strapped to their backs, leaving their hands free.

Barrabas led them down the valley and over the top of a low foothill. As they gained the summit, the radio tower's red beacon came into view. Nothing stood between them and their goal except a mile of jumbled foothills and a three-thousand-foot mountain. The mountain looked even steeper, hulking up out of the darkness.

Barrabas jogged on. There was coiled, untapped power in his legs; he sucked down great lungfuls of air. As they descended the low hill, he thought about another hill in another country. Capitol Hill. And the boys who sat on it like crows on a road-killed dog.

He had taken their money this time, but they had not bought him. He had already shown them such a thing was impossible. After Nam they had dangled something bright and shiny under his nose, the Congressional Medal of Honor. It was still somewhere in Washington, still in its box, unclaimed, gathering dust in a storeroom. Barrabas had the highest respect for that medal, for the men who had received it; he had no respect for the boys who had offered it to him. It had been a buy-back, pure and simple. Return to the fold, Nile Barrabas, and we will reward you.

Nile Barrabas preferred his reward in hell.

He knew on that terrible final day in Saigon, the last hours of the American pull out, that the only winners in the war had been the politicians. And he vowed they would never jerk his chain again. What he would do, he would do on his own terms, for his own reasons.

They took their first rest break behind a hilltop about halfway from the mountain.

"No sweat, huh?" Billy Two said softly.

"Funny man," Hayes answered. The perspiration was dripping off the tip of his nose and running in a steady stream down the middle of his back.

"Can it," the colonel told them.

They took their second break fifteen minutes later at the foot of the mountain. As they sat, Barrabas heard the Sikorsky way off. The sound was coming from the south. Gunther and Biondi would have dropped off the other two assault teams by now. They would climb five thousand feet and circle the camp five to eight miles out until they got the signal to come in for the pickup.

Barrabas checked his wristwatch. "We're right on schedule. We can take it nice and easy on the way up. No reason to push it."

The hard training on Málaga proved itself almost at once. They climbed with speed and confidence on the much gentler slope, following a line of least resistance that wound back and forth over boulders and rubble. Loose rock was the only thing that slowed their progress.

When they were one hundred yards from the summit, Barrabas stopped the men. They could see the upper third of the tower, its metalwork faintly backlit from the glow of the camp on the other side. Barrabas took a Starlite nightscope from his web belt and scanned the ground uphill. In the darkness between them and the foot of the antenna, some eighty yards away, was a heavily sandbagged dugout position. Though his angle of view was anything but optimum, he could clearly see a pair of machine guns stationed to sweep downslope. He recognized them as Iranian copies of the Czech ZB-30 in 7.92mm. There was movement along the upper edge of the stacked sandbags. Heads.

Billy Two was looking uphill, too, peering through the night sight of his M-21. "I count three," he whispered.

"Make it four," Barrabas corrected. "How many can you get?"

"At this angle, maybe two if I'm real lucky."

"That'll have to do. Give Claude and me ten minutes to work ourselves into position on their flanks, then open up whenever you're ready. Target of opportunity."

Barrabas and Hayes unshouldered packs and took up their weapons. Barrabas had replaced his XM-177's flash hider with an Interdynamics silencer. The magazine in the weapon and the spares tucked under his belt were loaded with specially constructed cartridges that kept muzzle velocity subsonic, below three hundred yards per second. Even without the silencer, the special 5.56mm rounds made about as much noise as a standard .22 Long Rifle and packed a lethal wallop to two hundred yards.

They synchronized watches, then Barrabas moved off to the left, slinging his rifle over his shoulder. He needed both hands free to climb with. When he was within thirty feet of the guard post, he stopped and checked his watch. The fluorescent numbers fell. Ten minutes on the nose. He quickly slipped out of the XM-177's sling, set the weapon on full-auto and released the safety.

Every muscle was tensed.

Ready.

Billy Two squinted through the nightscope. The very tip of a head showed tauntingly above the line of sandbags. Not nearly enough for him to risk a shot. Then he heard a gradually building droning sound. The Sikorsky was swinging past, way out there. The men in the guard post heard it, too. A figure jumped up on top of the wall of sandbags. He was looking up at the night sky and pointing.

Bless you, Dutchman, Billy Two thought as he laid the scope's cross hairs in the middle of the man's chest. Just before he squeezed the trigger a second sentry appeared, head and shoulders above the wall. Billy Two touched off the first shot and rode the soft recoil onto his next target. As he pulled the second time, his initial bullet scored. The man on the sandbags took a hit center chest, arms flying up over his head as he toppled backward into the dugout. The owner of the head and shoulders rose up slightly, instinctively.

Fatally.

Barrabas heard a solid whack. And then a groan. Before he could react there was another whack; then he was up and running.

Someone in the dugout yelped in surprise as the two dead men flopped inside.

Barrabas sprinted across the ten yards of flat, even ground. As he did so, the closest machine gun swung down on him. In his powerful hands the XM-177 was light and quick. He ripped off an 8-round burst. Over the muffled string of shots he could hear each fall of the firing pin. Yeah, it was quiet at his end.

Not so quiet at theirs. The 5.56mm tumblers clanged into metal, slapped into flesh, as he charged the barrier.

The guard post's fourth man panicked and took the back way out, vaulting the rear of the sandbagged pit, sprinting for the legs of the radio tower. For a second he was silhouetted against the glare of the camp lights. Barrabas tucked the butt of the XM-177 into his shoulder and put the sights between the runner's shoulder blades. Before he could squeeze off a burst, Hayes's silenced Uzi chugged from the right and the man went down hard in midstride.

They quickly checked the bodies, then climbed back down the hill to retrieve their packs. Five minutes later, Barrabas, Hayes and Billy Two looked down on the camp from the shadows at the base of the radio tower.

"At least you've got a path on this side," Billy Two said, pointing out the narrow goat trail that twisted down the steep slope.

"A nice, well-lit path," Hayes said ruefully.

"Don't worry about it," Barrabas told him, "they'll think we're just a couple of the boys.

Until we blow the living hell out of their fences.''

Billy Two tugged at a black cable running up one of the tower's legs. "Antenna wire, Colonel.''

"Right. That's for later.''

He left the two mercs stationed on the camp side of the mountaintop, watching for signals out on the plain that the two listening posts had been taken. He returned to the dark guard post and sat on the sandbag wall, staring at the opposite peak, awaiting the single pulse of light that would tell him the high ground was theirs.

LIAM O'TOOLE CRAWLED the last twenty feet of open space between the rock outcrop and the hilltop dugout. He lay on his back beside the layered sandbags, listening to a heated three-way conversation in Pharsee, a language he could not make heads nor tails of.

Then a light came on inside the guard post. Beams leaked through the cracks and gaps in the stacked bags. The argument continued.

It was time to end it.

O'Toole rolled up and leaned over the top sandbag, clutching a silenced CAR.

The six men in the fortified pit gawked at him.

Dead in the water.

Lee and Chen rose up from the other side.

One of the Pasdars slowly raised his hands in surrender. The rest dived for their weapons. Four seconds of absolute mayhem followed as

Uzis and XM-177 cut down the scrambling Iranians. The Pasdar with his hands in the air had a sudden change of heart as hot gore splattered his face and chest. He jumped in the direction of a G-3 assault rifle and a walkie-talkie.

Both were deadly.

O'Toole stopped him with a 3-round burst.

After they had made sure that all the guardsmen were down for good, O'Toole took out his flashlight and blinked it once in the direction of the radio tower. The message: west peak under control.

A light answered. One blink.

Message: proceed.

"Okay," O'Toole said to Lee and Chen, "take off." He watched as they shouldered packs and weapons and started downslope at a brisk clip. They had the hardest hump of all. It was the penalty they paid for being in the best shape of any of the mercs.

O'Toole set up shop on the edge of the summit overlooking the camp. His killzone was so well-lit that he had no need of the Starlite scope on the M-21. He removed it and clamped on an adjustable ranging telescope. He knew Billy Two would be doing the same thing.

O'Toole settled down in a prone position behind the bipod-mounted weapon and picked a target, one of the several that were his primary responsibility: the farthest of the two guard towers on his side of the camp. There were a pair of men inside. He chose the one behind the Iranian Model 30 machine gun. Using the ART's magnification ring, he adjusted the stadia, two horizontal lines at the top and bottom of the field of view. When the stadia bracketed the man from belt line to head, O'Toole was aiming the rifle at the midpoint of his chest. The M-21 would hit what it was aimed at, too. Its ART was ballistically calibrated to the USM118 NATO ammo he was using.

Having zeroed in on his most distant targets, O'Toole quickly worked his way back, sighting in on men moving around the compound, finishing off with the guard tower nearest him. Satisfied, he sat up and set out extra loaded magazines of 7.62mm ammunition.

Then he leaned his back against a boulder and stared across the saddle at the far peak, waiting for the signal to begin.

DR. LEE HATTON was beginning to wonder if Al Chen was really human. The man was relentless. His pace across the plain was even faster than their headlong descent of the mountain. Every so often he looked back at her, asking without words if she needed a rest. Lee was not about to give in to her aching joints and throbbing muscles. Too much depended on their getting to the westernmost listening post on schedule.

It was SOP that every hour each of the guard posts and LPs had to check in with the camp.

From the moment Barrabas, Hayes and Billy Two took the radio-tower outpost, she and Chen had no more than fifty-nine minutes to cover three and a half miles of broken ground.

As she jogged, laden down with weapons and explosives, she thought about her father, the general, and found a reason to smile. If he were alive, he would have found nothing remarkable in what she was doing. The general would have expected no less from a Hatton, any Hatton.

As they came even with the rear of the camp, five hundred yards out on the plain to its west, Chen held up his hand for a slow down.

At first Lee thought she was grateful for the break, then her body reacted to the heat buildup. The perspiration felt like it was squirting out of her skin. She took some water.

They walked carefully for twenty-five yards or so, then Chen leaned down and pointed to something on the ground. It was a small microphone on a stake. One of the listening post's ears.

Chen cut the connecting wire and held it in his hand. He pointed in the direction the wire was coming from.

She nodded. They would follow the wire back to its source, using the listening post's own sensors to locate it. The Iranian LPs were simply holes dug in the plain, surrounded by low piles of rock. In daylight they would have been hard to pick out. At night they were close to impossible.

They had gone only a short distance when

Chen stopped again. He pulled and cut a second microphone hidden along the line of the one they were following. It was meant to defend against just what they were doing.

Chen unslung his M-21, turned on the Starlite scope and scanned the area ahead. With her naked eyes, Lee could not see more than seventy-five yards in the direction opposite the camp. And in the seventy-five yards of gently downward sloping plain, she could pick out no single rock outcrop that looked more promising than any other.

Even with the nightscope, Chen had the same kind of luck. He slung the weapon again and gestured for her to remain where she was. Then he set off to the right, moving slowly.

She knew what he was up to. The LP's wires were set out like the spokes of a wheel, radiating from a central hub. All they had to do was find two of the wires. At the point ahead where the wires came together they would find the LP.

At the very edge of her range of vision, Chen knelt down. She did not actually see him shoulder the M-21. Nor did she hear him shoot. She did see him jump up and start running in the direction of the LP. She followed, her silenced Uzi in her hands.

He was already down in the foxhole when she arrived.

"Got 'em both," he said, turning over the limp forms of two Pasdars. One of them still had his headset on.

Lee took out her flashlight and signaled the peak. Now all they had to do was dash back and provide critical flanking fire on the west side of the camp perimeter.

As Chen started to climb out of the pit, a man's voice broke the silence. It came from the plain behind Lee. The speaker asked an urgent question.

In Pharsee.

BOONE JAMMED the nightscope's rubber eyepiece against his eye socket. If there were two guys in the rock-rimmed hole seventy yards away, you could not prove it by him.

"Rattle their cage a little," Boone whispered to Nanos and Beck. He waved them to either side of him.

They picked up softball-sized rocks and chucked them as far as they could, to the left and right of the LP's position. Out in the darkness, the rocks clunked once, clattered and were still.

There was no movement from the pit.

Boone knew he had gotten their attention, though. The adrenaline would be pumping up a storm as ears strained to hear more. He waved at Nanos and Beck to do it again.

Rocks clunked.

Boone grinned to himself. A pair of single clunks were not the kinds of sounds the Pasdars had been trained to expect. The tramp of an invading force would sound like a herd of elephants through the sensitive microphones.

Two helmeted heads raised above the protective ring of piled rock.

Whatever the strange noises were, the Pasdars were sure they were not dangerous.

Boone grinned again. The Islamic Revolutionary Guards were not dead sure. They were sure dead.

The M-21 bucked once, then again. The 7.62mm NATO slugs whined away. There were two more lonely clunks in the night. They sounded different, though: metallic; hollow; the sound of helmets, bone and brain yielding to 165 grains of lead.

The SOBs ran for the LP and dragged the corpses out. Beck signaled the colonel and received an answer at once.

Attack.

15

"Say, who are those two?" the Pasdar machine gunner said, standing up from behind his weapon and pointing.

The other Pasdar in the guard tower raised his binoculars, focused and his jaw went slack. The heavily armed men casually walking down the path from the radio antenna were not Islamic Revolutionary Guards. They were not even Iranians. One was black. The other was white. Even his hair.

He spat out a curse, whirling around to grab at the walkie-talkie hanging on a nail behind him. His hand never closed on it. Something hit him hard in the lower back. For a split second he thought the machine gunner had given him a kick. Then his legs gave way. As he dropped to his knees the pain began, and he knew he had been struck by a bullet. He opened his mouth to scream and blood gushed out of his throat like vomit. The machine gunner would sound the alarm, he thought as he toppled onto his face. He had to sound the alarm. Then something above and to his left exploded. He was sprayed with sticky wetness and bits of bone.

There would be no alarm.

BARRABAS LED THE WAY down the hill. The XM-177 slung on his back no longer had a silencer attached. They were beyond the point of worrying about noise. He and Hayes carried M-79 grenade launchers loaded with high-explosive projectiles.

Barrabas knew how obvious the two of them would be to anyone in camp bothering to look uphill. He was counting on the fact that only the men in the guard towers would pay any real attention to who came and went on the mountain, and that only those men would be likely to have binoculars.

Even as they descended, Billy Two and O'Toole were eliminating the personnel in all four guard towers from their high-ground positions. Barrabas had complete confidence in their marksmanship. He was betting his life on it.

The Iranian camp below was now cut off, an island in the midst of its own country. Barrabas had cut the radio antenna. The LPs were gone. The only road out was under their control. Men moved around the compound, handling routine duties. As far as they knew, it was still business as usual.

Barrabas counted thirty men outside the bunker.

No, even as he looked a man in a camouflage uniform fell near the bunker entrance. He did not get up.

One of the Pasdars stationed at the machine gun emplacement beside the entrance jumped up and ran to the downed soldier. As he leaned over, something kicked up a puff of dirt a foot behind him. The Pasdar looked around, then suddenly clutched at his chest and toppled.

Things were getting serious.

"This is close enough," Barrabas said, shouldering his XM-177. "Let's hit it."

He fired an instant before Hayes. The 40mm HE projectiles arced gracefully downrange. Hellfire bloomed among the fences. They quickly reloaded and laid two more rounds on the same spot. Then Barrabas charged straight downslope, into the spiraling cloud of smoke and dust.

THE MAN STANDING BEHIND LEE repeated his question.

Her mind was working a mile a minute. Maybe it was a man's name, she thought. One of the guys who were supposed to be on duty at the LP. It was lucky that her hair was black and cut short, that her pale skin was concealed by the combat makeup, or there would not have been a query from behind, only a bullet.

She stole a quick glance back. As she did, she shifted her Uzi on its shoulder strap, bringing the pistol grip into her right hand. There were four men standing less than forty feet away—four men with three shovels apiece propped on their shoulders, and assault rifles in their hands, pointing downward.

What they were doing with the extra shovels was a puzzle Lee did not have time to consider. With her left hand she pulled the Uzi's top cocking knob back until it locked in place, then with her right thumb pushed the fire-selector lever forward, from safe to full-auto.

Another man shouted something to Chen, who crouched in the foxhole.

Chen did not answer, either.

Behind her, shovels clattered to the ground. Footsteps approached. There was no cover except the foxhole, and she would be dead before she reached it. They would expect her to go that way. Only a maniac would try anything different.

Lee had already decided it was wild-and-crazy time when the night's stillness was shattered. A flash of light and a dull whump erupted from the camp. She moved as if the explosion was a well-rehearsed cue, diving away from the foxhole.

Gunfire blazed as she swung around the silenced Uzi. The Pasdars were shooting, but not at her. Al Chen was firing from the foxhole, drawing the heat away from her. He cut down two of the guardsmen before the ungodly hail of bullets caught up with him.

Lee opened up from a prone position, sweeping her sights across the Pasdaran duo as she held the Uzi's trigger pinned. Dozens of chest hits blew the Iranians backward. They went down hard and stayed down.

She scrambled over to the LP. Chen was there, on his back. She fumbled for her flashlight. "It's going to be okay, Al," she said. "It's going to be okay."

One good look at him told her it was not.

"Son of a bitch!" she cried, slamming the flashlight down on the rocks. All her years of professional training, her experience in combat could not do Al Chen any good.

He had taken five rounds through the face.

The man had died for her.

There would be time for tears later. If she survived. She turned and ran for the camp.

Al Chen was dead. . . .

LIEUTENANT YAZDI had gathered a few of his favorite noncoms in the metal shop and was sharing with them his execution experience.

"They squealed like pigs," Yazdi said through a grin as big as all outdoors.

One of the noncoms made a shrill pig sound, much to the amusement of the others.

Yazdi raised his hand, index finger extended, thumb crooked back and fired an imaginary bullet through the sergeant's eye.

A terrible roar from above put an abrupt end to the fun. The bunker shuddered. Ceiling tiles rained down on them. The lights flickered and went out.

The darkness was filled with angry shouts.

Yazdi bellowed. "Get the lights back on!"

Power was restored almost at once.

The lieutenant charged out into the hallway, knocking aside Pasdars who accidentally blocked his path. He stuck his head into the open doorway of the communications room. "The guard posts?" he demanded of a visibly shaken radio operator. "Any word from the guard posts?"

"Nothing, sir. They do not respond."

The conclusion was unavoidable.

"Radio for help immediately!"

"Sir, the radio is out. It isn't sending or receiving."

"Oh, God," Yazdi groaned. He turned and shouted down the long hallway, "We're under attack! Seal up the bunker! Seal it quickly!"

As he raced back to his quarters to get his weapons, the lieutenant cursed the luck of Mohamadi Razod.

Luck that had allowed him to escape this ultimate catastrophe.

NATE BECK SPRINTED full out down the dirt road. On either side of him were Nanos and Boone. His legs felt funny, like he had big soft pillows strapped to the bottom of his feet. And his head felt light, too.

Not since the first time he got laid, in the back

seat of a buddy's father's Caddy after a B'nai Brith teen social, had there been such thunder raging in his veins.

They were one hundred yards from the gates when grenades exploded on the camp perimeter.

"Do it," Boone said, stopping.

Beck shouldered an M-79. So did Nanos. They fired at the same instant. It was only after the projectile was away that Beck realized he had not bothered to aim it.

One HE shell burst the first gate to bits.

Somebody was way off with the other.

A guard tower twenty yards off to the right exploded in flame.

"Jesus, Nate!" Nanos exclaimed. "Was that you?"

Beck did not answer. His face was burning all the way to the tips of his ears. Nanos had just paraphrased the very same question asked of him in the back seat of Mr. Goldstein's El Dorado. He cracked the Bloop gun's breech and stuffed in another 40mm shell. Easy, he told himself. Take it nice and easy.

As it had been eighteen years before, the second time was a charm.

Two explosions. One for each of the camp's remaining gates.

They switched M-79s for Uzis and raced for the shattered barriers. No sooner were they through them than they came under heavy fire.

Beck had read a lot about wars, gunfights and

the like. The closest he had gotten to the real thing was to serve in the Air Force as a communications expert. Some of the books had explained that in combat a guy lived a thousand years in a few miserable seconds. He finally knew what that meant.

It took at least five lifetimes for them to cross the open ground between the blown gates and the first storage dome. As they ran, bullets whipped around them, ricocheting off the rocks at their feet. The whole time, Beck kept wondering how they could miss. Were they such bad shots? They would have to get lucky sooner or later.

To Beck's astonishment, he, Boone and Nanos made it safely to the cover of the storage building. Bullets drilled into the far side of the prefab metal dome in a steady stream. The Pasdars had found something they could hit with consistency.

"Jesus, we've got fire coming at us from both sides," Nanos said. "Where the hell are Lee and Chen? They're supposed to be taking some of the heat off."

"We can't worry about them," Boone said. He sneaked a peek around the dome and ducked back quickly. "We've got to mop up the opposition and rendezvous with the colonel. There's six to ten shooters on our right, in the motor-pool area. They're in among all those oil drums. You guys hit 'em. I'll keep the ones on the right off your asses."

Beck shrugged out of his pack, and from it he

dug out a half-dozen loaded Uzi stick magazines. He stuck five of them in under his web belt; the sixth he held in his left hand, ready for a quick reload.

While Nanos was rooting around in his pack, Beck took a fast look around the corner. The motor pool contained a few jeeps and trucks. There was a repair area roofed over to provide shelter from the sun; it had no walls or floor. Beside that structure were about two hundred metal drums. Some of them had no lids. Some of those had Pasdars inside.

Nanos grabbed Beck's shoulder and pulled him back. A volley of slugs slammed into the dome and skipped off the stones where he had been.

"Let's see if that oil will burn," the Greek said. He yanked the pin on the hand grenade he held, let the grip safety plink off, then stepped out into the lane of fire and threw.

He had a hell of an arm.

The Pasdars who had been shooting recognized the stance and ducked.

There was a solid thunderclap report and a half-dozen empty fifty-gallon drums jumped into the air like beer cans.

"It's not burning," Nanos said as he stepped back.

The gunfire from the motor-pool area resumed.

"But the gas sure as hell will," he went on.

"There's a big red tank over in the repair bay. It's downhill from there to the drums."

"Barrabas was wrong," Beck said, "about where you keep your brains."

"Naw, he was right. I'm hung like King Kong." The Greek turned to Boone and said, "Can you manage to keep 'em down in their barrels long enough for us to cross the open ground?"

"Yeah, I sure can, now. Hear that?"

From off to the west, mixed in among the short bursts of auto-rifle fire, came the sound of ripping canvas. It was an unmuffled Uzi spitting 9mm lead at six hundred fifty rounds per minute.

"Lee and Chen. It's about time," Nanos said. "Me first, Nate."

Beck followed right on the Greek's heels as he dashed across the stones. The 5.56mm bullets, Boone's covering fire, whined over their heads and to either side of them. When they reached the drums, they stopped and knelt down. Ahead, in crooked rows, were the two hundred oil drums. Each was potentially a hiding place for a fanatic. The path to the repair bay and gas tank skirted the edge of the drums.

"Wanna go home?" Nanos said to his companion.

"You got it," Beck said.

"Let's get this over with, then." Nanos raised himself to a crouch and started moving along the line of barrels.

Beck was two steps behind.

They had gone no more than a dozen yards when Beck heard something move to his left, in among the cans. Nanos was facing the other way, his back to the sound.

"Look out!" Beck cried. He threw a shoulder into the Greek's back, knocking him out of the line of fire. The only trouble was, it was too late to save himself.

The Pasdar popped out of a drum two rows away. His Heckler and Koch 32 assault rifle was aimed at Beck's heart. The guy was smiling. He had reason to. Beck's Uzi was still pointed at the sky.

The H&K 32 stuttered. Four .308-1 caliber slugs slammed against the muscle of Nate's chest. It was like being hit with a sledgehammer over and over. Each impact knocked him back a full foot.

The Pasdar had expected the bullets to do a whole lot more than that. When the skinny guy did not fall, he was momentarily stunned.

Despite the force of the bullets, Beck somehow managed to keep his balance. He got the Uzi's muzzle down and cut loose with a horrendous sustained burst of fire that practically beheaded the man in the oil drum.

Then he ducked down. He touched the holes in the front of his camouflage shirt.

"That Kevlar's great stuff," Nanos said.

"Hate to see what I look like underneath it, though.''

''Let's get out of here before you have to save my life again.''

When they reached the repair bay, Nanos told Beck to get behind a jeep. "You keep 'em busy while I hose 'em down.''

Beck potshotted at the rows of oil drums. When he looked back, the Greek had freed the gas tank's nozzle and was squirting a feeble stream of the liquid down the gentle slope. At the rate it was going, it would take a half hour for the gas to reach the farthest drum. The problem was, the tank had no pump on it. It was raised above the ground and worked by gravity.

"Screw this,'' Nanos said, dropping the nozzle. He ran over to the cluttered workbench and began frantically searching among the tools. Finally he found what he was looking for. He showed Beck the single-bladed ax. "Behold, the Iranian speed wrench,'' he said.

Nanos rubbed spit on the blade to prevent sparks, then attacked the lower portion of the gas tank in a frenzy, punching great slashes through the metal, sending a torrent of high-octane fuel gushing downslope. Beck admired the way the Greek worked, nimbly avoiding the flow of gas as he cut the tank from end to end.

Nanos dragged some greasy rags through a gas puddle, then the two men moved to a safe distance. The Greek lit the rags and tossed them up against the ruptured tank. It whooshed into a ball of orange flame. The fire leaped along the ground, spreading in a matter of seconds to encompass the drums.

Nanos, Beck and Boone picked off the smart ones, the Pasdars who chose to die before they burned.

BARRABAS VAULTED the downed fences. Amid the smoke and dust, white-hot arcs of electricity zapped and sputtered along the ground. He avoided the shorted-out high-tension wires and burst through the choking cloud into the compound.

The first Pasdar he met he almost ran over.

The sight of Barrabas suddenly appearing out of the swirling haze froze the Iranian in his tracks. Before he could recover and bring his homegrown version of a Soviet PPSH-41 submachine gun to bear, Barrabas put a round through his head.

It was not think time. It was act time. Will time. Nothing could stop him from gaining the sandbagged entrance to the bunker. Nothing. He raced straight into the teeth of the light-machine gun guarding the bunker, his CAR bucking between his hands as he rained 5.56mm slugs against the fortified position.

The machine gunner got off only one burst. And it was wild. Either Barrabas had taken him out with a lucky shot or, more likely, one of the snipers, O'Toole or Billy Two, had nailed him from above.

As Barrabas closed on the bunker entrance he knew it was going to be tight. He could see the tops of the bombproof steel doors swinging shut. Claude Hayes, a much faster runner, drew abreast of him. He could see the doors, too. He veered off to the right.

Barrabas snatched a concussion grenade from his web belt and pulled the pin with his teeth. As he turned past the edge of the sandbags and hit the long ramp leading down, he let the grip safety pop off.

The double doors were almost closed. A scant foot separated them. Barrabas knew he was not going to make it.

Hayes jumped the sandbag barrier at ground level near the entrance, dropped twelve feet and came down on the ramp ahead of the colonel. With an effort as brilliant as it was desperate, the black man jammed the butt of his M-79 into the gap, holding it wedged inches apart.

For a second, the men on the other side of the doors kept pulling, not realizing what had happened. It was long enough for Barrabas to reach the gap and gently roll the concussion grenade through. Then he and Hayes spun aside, throwing their backs against the doors, bracing with their legs, keeping the M-79 trapped where it was.

A hand stuck out of the gap; in it was an automatic pistol.

All Hayes and Barrabas could do was watch.

"Now! Now!" Hayes shouted.

The hand turned at the wrist, trying to get the barrel aimed.

"For God's sake, now!"

The shock of the explosion through the heavy steel doors rattled their brains. On the other side, in the confined space of the bunker corridor, it was a hundred times worse. The hand with the gun had disappeared, as had all apparent resistance.

Barrabas quickly climbed to the top of the sandbags and waved at the peaks, calling down O'Toole and Billy Two. As he turned back, he saw the rest of his soldiers coming toward him on the run. Behind them, the camp was burning, bodies were burning.

It was a vision straight from hell.

16

When the stun grenade detonated, Lieutenant Yazdi was rushing to join the men at the bunker doors. There was only one sandbag barrier between him and the concussion. It rocked the entire corridor, blowing him off his feet. He lay on the hallway floor unable to clear the roaring in his ears, to shake the spinning in his head.

An Islamic Revolutionary Guard staggered around the sandbag wedge, hands and arms extended in a blind grope. He was dusted with pulverized cement. Blood poured from his ears, nose and eyes; it bubbled from the corners of his mouth.

"Watch out," the lieutenant groaned.

The Pasdar stumbled over Yazdi, falling across him. His forehead hit the floor with a solid thunk. Then he began to twitch.

In his dazed state it took the lieutenant a few seconds to understand why the back of the man's skull looked the way it did—concave instead of convex. With a curse he shoved the fresh corpse off his legs and scrambled to his feet.

"Pasdars! Regroup!" he shouted. His voice

sounded shrill and thin. Panic clutched tightly at his throat. There was the taste of blood in his mouth.

Other men were shouting, too, shouting and screaming.

The unthinkable had happened. The bunker entrance was in the control of an attacking force. The only chance the defenders had was to pull back and pull together. He grabbed a PPSH-41 submachine gun from the floor, charged the bolt, swung the shrouded barrel up and unleashed a deafening 900-round-per-minute burst into the ceiling. It froze the stampeding Pasdars in their tracks.

"Retreat!" he yelled, waving them to the rear of the complex.

Men scurried out of the mess hall opposite him.

"Lieutenant," a wild-eyed noncom said, "there are still men in the barracks."

The dormitory for the soldiers was on the other side of the first sandbag radiation barrier, now cut off from the main corridor and retreat by a lane of fire from the steel entry doors.

Yazdi jammed the snout of the submachine gun against the sergeant's stomach. "I said retreat!"

The sergeant backed away, nodding.

The guardsmen ran down the zigzag hallway, stopping at the armory on Yazdi's command to gather weapons and ammunition. On the far side of the officers' quarters and communications room, the main corridor was crossed at a right angle by another hall, like the top bar of a T. This rear hallway housed the rad lab, the electronics lab, the metal shop and explosives storage room. Like the main corridor, it was partially blocked by floor-to-ceiling sandbag wedges, creating a zigzag effect.

The lieutenant quickly divided his fifty-man force. He sent half the troops and a sergeant toward the rad lab at the far end of the passageway. They took up a position around the corner of the sandbags shielding the rad-lab door. From there they could see the opening of the main corridor and the sandbags piled against its far wall.

Yazdi took the rest of the Pasdars the other way, to a similar structure that protected the explosives room at the opposite end of the passage. From his position, the lieutenant could see not only the main corridor opening, but, because there were no sandbags on the other side of the hall facing him, he could also see about fifteen feet of wall.

He felt a lot more confident than he had at first. He had placed his troops so they could protect each other. And if worse came to worst and they had to retreat even farther, they could barricade themselves in the rad lab and explosives room.

Lieutenant Yazdi had foreseen the worst as a very real possibility. That was why he had picked that end of the hallway for himself.

The explosives room had a heavy steel door.

"WHERE'S CHEN?" Barrabas said as the SOBs regrouped outside the bunker doors.

Lee Hatton just shook her head.

No one said anything.

Their eyes sought either the middle distance or the ground; no glances were exchanged.

Each was alone with what he felt, alone with direct and irrefutable evidence of his own mortality.

Only fools look on war as a game.

A game has rules. And lost pieces are resurrected at the end of play.

The SOBs were a lot of things, some distasteful, some worse; but they were not fools. When one of them fell in battle, they all died a little bit.

And their commander died the most of all.

In the dancing firelight Barrabas's face was a terrifying mask. All hard angles and jutting bone. And behind the heavy, narrowed lids his eyes spoke of savagery long past, of savagery yet to come.

The somber silence was shattered by the chatter of an Uzi. Claude Hayes knelt in front of the steel doors, holding the right one open just wide enough to shoot through.

"Colonel, we've got some movement in there," he said. Then he cursed and the Uzi chattered some more, spitting a bright string of spent brass. "There's a doorway on the right, just inside," Hayes went on. "Guys are trying to jump from there, across the gap, to the cover of a sandbag wall."

"We can't wait for O'Toole and Billy Two," Barrabas said. "We've got to make our move, now. Nanos, Beck and Boone, you take the first door. Lee, Hayes and I will lay down cover, then move ahead."

The black man opened fire again, then the Uzi came up empty. He pulled back and shut the door.

An insane volley of bullets clanged against the other side.

Hayes grinned as he cracked a fresh mag into his submachine gun. "I think I've pissed 'em off."

"Let's give 'em another headache," Nanos said, jerking a stun grenade from his web belt. He yanked the pin and when Boone opened the door, he underhanded the bomb through the crack. He watched it bounce once on the floor, then hop inside the doorway on the right.

Boone slammed the door.

The bunker rocked from the explosion.

Before the thunderclap faded, Beck, Nanos and Boone poured into the corridor, their boots slipping on the heaped bodies of the men caught by the first grenade. The fallen Pasdars were more than stunned; they were very dead. Small space, big bang.

Boone did not pause at the barracks doorway. He dashed straight into the dust, smoke and, he sincerely hoped, confusion of his enemies. He ducked to the right and dropped to a crouch beside the end of a row of battered metal footlockers.

Once through the door, Nanos and Beck cut the other way, diving for the dubious cover of a four-level bunk bed that stuck out from the wall.

Ahead of them was tier upon tier of bunks, a forest of metal in the low-ceilinged room. The narrow beds were unmade. Aisle-spanning clotheslines were hung with laundry, some dirty, some wet, some both. On the walls, the lockers, the bed frames, the furious likeness of a bearded ancient scowled down on them.

"Damn! What is that smell?" Nanos muttered as he swept the sights of his XM-177 back and forth.

"You sweat what you eat," Beck told him.

"Can't say much about their taste in pinups, either," Boone said. "It definitely leans toward the old and crusty."

"Shut up. You guys are making me sick."

Nothing moved in the room but dust. Dust drifting down. Behind the hanging blankets, under the bunks, there were hundreds of hiding places.

"Don't know about you," Boone said, "but I've got this real powerful feeling we've got possum back in there. We just need to chase 'em out."

"Too bad we didn't bring the hounds," Nanos said.

"I'll be the dog," Boone said. He straightened up and slowly moved in front of the row of lockers.

He got maybe twenty steps before the possums showed themselves.

Auto-rifle fire roared from the center of the mass of bunks. Heavy slugs slammed and rattled the lockers. Boone spun and dived back the way he had come, trying desperately to avoid the line of lead stitching toward him.

Then it was "mad minute" time.

Nanos and Beck from the floor, Barrabas and Hayes from the doorway, all cut loose at once. The full-auto hail crashed through the bunk-bed forest. The Iranian possums shot back.

Barrabas emptied one twenty-round magazine and started on a second. The din of gunfire was so furious that it was impossible to hear the bodies hitting the floor. They could be seen, though—dark forms slumping down between the aisles, dropping limply from the upper bunks.

When the firing from the other side ceased, when there was no more movement among the blankets and bunk frames, the SOBs stopped shooting.

The smell of cordite was thick, acrid. The floor was littered with hundreds of spent rounds.

"Oh, Jesus," Nanos said as he looked over at the footlockers.

Boone was down.

The Greek started toward him, but Barrabas stepped in his way. "No, let Lee handle it," he said. "You guys check the Pasdars, on the double. We can't proceed until this room is a hundred percent clean."

Lee Hatton was already bending over the fallen man. Boone was lying on his face, and she did not try to turn him. She could see his wound. He had been hit in the back of the head. The track of the slug ran parallel to his shoulders, not very deep, but deep enough. Part of his skull was blasted away. She took a pulse at the side of his throat.

"Dammit, he's alive," she said, drawing back.

Barrabas knelt down beside the unconscious man. "Bottom line, doc."

"His heart's still beating strong. If he lives he's going to be a vegetable. No way around it."

Barrabas waited until the others had completed their body check, then said, "Lee, get out of here. Beck, Nanos, you, too." He reached for the butt of his Browning Hi-Power.

Lee stayed his hand. "No, Nile," she said, "this is my job."

Barrabas looked into her black eyes.

"Chen saved my life out there and I couldn't help him. I can still do something for Boone, even if it's only to give him a way out."

It was right and Barrabas knew it—right that the last person in this life to touch Wiley Drew Boone was a beautiful woman.

"Come on," he said to the mercs, "let's clean out the rest of this dung heap." At the door he glanced back. Lee already had her medical kit open. She was loading a syringe.

Out in the hallway, Barrabas and the others were joined by O'Toole and Billy Two.

"We're down to seven," Barrabas told them.

O'Toole looked around, counting faces. "Jesus, not Lee," he said.

"No, not Lee," the woman answered from the dormitory doorway. There were streaks in her camouflage makeup from where she had hurriedly wiped away tears. She cracked back the cocking knob of her Uzi. "What the hell is this, a convention or something?"

No quarter asked. No quarter given.

Barrabas could not help but smile as he led the unit forward. Dr. Hatton was one fine soldier. He waved O'Toole and Billy Two over to the peak of the next sandbag wedge where they could defend against a counterattack from forces deeper in the bunker. Then Barrabas and the rest of the SOBs slipped quietly into the mess hall.

It was even bleaker than the barracks. And it did not smell any better. There were rows of folding tables and chairs. There were big posters of the bearded wonder on the walls. At the rear of the room, near the cooking area, a half-dozen tables were overturned to form a barrier.

Barrabas knew what was coming. He signaled for his mercs to quickly spread out.

The Pasdars in the mess were cut off from their fellows.

Doomed.

But bound by their own creed to die with glory.

With piercing screams of exultation, ten Islamic Revolutionary Guards jumped the flimsy barricades, their H&Ks and Uzis spitting death.

Barrabas fired from the hip, tempering the shrieking zealots' passion with .223-caliber downers. Pills of tumbling lead that gouged away great hunks of flesh, slicing through bone, sinew, blood vessel. He hit the front runner in the right shoulder, turning him, then hit him again in the middle of the back and left shoulder. The man continued to spin ahead, even as his rubber legs tangled and sent him sprawling.

What was happening was an obscenity called the "human wave." The Pasdars first over the barricade ran straight into the withering fire, driving forward, absorbing slugs so the men behind them could get even closer. And the men behind them closer still. The guardsmen were so

pumped up that only the most devastating
wounds stopped them.

The din of screams and automatic gunfire was
nerve-shattering. Barrabas emptied his XM-177.
There was no time to reload. He shifted the car-
bine to his left hand and jerked his Browning Hi-
Power free of hip leather. He pumped five 9mm
rounds into the throat of an oncoming Iranian,
then stepped aside and let the running corpse
slam face first into the wall.

It was over.

Less than seven seconds of real time had
elapsed.

Barrabas surveyed the Pasdar dead. Every one
of them had made it more than halfway across
the room. Three had made it all the way to the
wall.

"What keeps these guys up?" Nanos wondered.

It was a question all of the SOBs were asking
themselves. The men inside the bunker were
fighting with a hundred times the intensity of
those they had encountered above. It was obvious what was driving them: fear. The Pasdars
were cornered rats, clawing and scratching to
keep control of their own nasty little nest.

Barrabas discarded the empty mag and
snapped in a fresh one. It had been hairy, all
right—hairy and then some. He looked at the
faces of his soldiers. Grim, determined faces.
They had held together in spite of what had been

thrown at them; they had stood their ground as if rooted to it. It was synergy in action: the effectiveness of the team is greater than the sum of its individual members. The SOBs were a precision-honed killing machine, not because they were committed to some suicidal mystic-religious dogma, but because they were committed to each other, each determined not to be the weak link that brought the others down.

As they exited the mess hall, Billy Two and O'Toole moved ahead of them, rounding the sandbags and easing down the hallway. They passed two more barriers without meeting resistance. They moved through the armory, communication room and officers' quarters and found no one.

In front of them was the sandbag wedge that blocked off two-thirds of the end of the main hallway. O'Toole put his back to the barrier and peeked around it, down the rear corridor. He pulled back fast.

"Can't see anything, Colonel. Just a pile of sandbags across the way. And the door down farther against the back wall."

Barrabas opened his mouth to speak.

Something small and black bumped into the left-hand wall, then skittered in front of them, spinning on its side like a top. A perfect bank shot. Only it was not a top.

It was a hand grenade.

Billy Two was the closest to it. There was no time to bend down and pick it up. He used his XM-177 like a hockey stick, batting the grenade back against the wall, making it rebound the way it had come, to the other side of the piled barrier.

LIEUTENANT YAZDI'S EYES widened in horror as the grenade he had just pitched came rolling back into the corridor. He hurled himself to the floor, diving for the protection of the sandbags at his end of the hallway, covering the back of his head with his hands.

The detonation was earsplitting.

It signaled the end of Yazdi's hastily drawn up defense plan. He struggled to his feet. Men at the other end of the hall were down. Even as he looked others fell, those far enough away to avoid being blown off their feet, but not far enough away to avoid the red-hot spines of steel. The sergeant was dead; so were half the Pasdars at the rad lab. They had been poised to charge the invaders as soon as the grenade went off. Unfortunately for them, the grenade had rolled only a few feet back down the corridor before exploding.

The survivors at the far end were trying to help their dying comrades.

"Back!" Yazdi shouted. "Leave them and pull back!"

The lieutenant then turned and, ignoring the

cries of the wounded around him, scrambled for the safety of the explosives room.

THE THUNDERCLAP KNOCKED the SOBs to the floor, but the heavy wedge of sandbags protected them from flying shrapnel.

Barrabas was the first to his feet. He pulled a grenade from his web belt. "Nanos, southpaw one for me to the right."

The Greek put his back to the left-hand wall and edged out until the sandbags no longer obstructed his toss. He and Barrabas yanked pins at the same moment, counting down, then throwing together. They crisscrossed grenades. The colonel threw his to the left, bouncing it off the sandbag barrier into the corridor. Nanos chucked his deep down the right side, making it bounce off the door to the metal shop and drop in front of the explosives room.

Yazdi was already behind the closed steel door when the hallway rocked from the double explosion.

"A barricade, quickly!" he shrieked at the dozen surviving guardsmen.

Under his direction, they moved heavy crates against the inward opening door.

They need not have bothered.

The moment the explosions faded, the SOBs charged the back hallway. On the rad-lab side, because of the sandbag barriers, the opposing field of fire was only about ten feet wide.

They crossed it without drawing so much as a shot.

For good reason.

There was no longer anybody at home.

The corridor was choked with corpses, whole and in parts. The walls were blackened by smoke and heat, splashed with red.

And the only sound the SOBs could hear was like the passing of time as sand leaked out through slits and slashes in the heaped bags.

Hayes and Nanos turned and ran to the opposite end of the hallway. Sand from broken bags had shifted down, partially covering the tangled mass of gristle and gore that had been ten living men. Sand could not conceal the overpowering stench of death in front of the explosives-room door.

Hayes touched the door's metal hasp, cursing as his fingers were burned, then used a shirt cuff to close it. Nanos jammed his boot knife down through the hasp's ring.

"Gotcha!" the Greek shouted, kicking the door with the sole of his boot.

LIEUTENANT YAZDI did not understand the English slang. He took it for a cry of impotent rage. He harangued his men who had flinched at the thud on the other side of the door. "There is nothing they can do to us, now. No way they can get in. The entire bunker will collapse before that door will fall down."

One of the Pasdars spoke up. "Isn't it our duty to fight to the death? There are enough explosives in this room to kill the invaders if we set them off."

Yazdi glowered at the man. "Idiot, someone must survive to tell the world what happened. That is our only duty."

"Somebody's talking in there," Nanos said. "I can hear it, but I can't make it out."

"Come on," Hayes said.

Nanos gave the door a final kick for good measure.

Barrabas and the others had already rounded the last barrier at the rad-lab end of the corridor. The door to the lab was shut, too, but it was made of reinforced wood. Keeping out of the line of fire, his back to the wall, Billy Two tried the knob.

The door's center exploded outward, splintering as a barrage of small-arms fire smashed through it.

Billy Two blew on his fingertips. "Well, Colonel?"

The jagged hole was softball-sized. Through it, Barrabas could see the top of a desk the Pasdars had shoved against the back of the door. He could not risk chucking a frag or concussion grenade through the hole in the door because of the equipment inside. He could not use teargas, either, because he was not sure they could ventilate the bunker adequately afterward. Beck had to be able to see to rig the bomb. If they were going to do it, it had to be done the hard way, with minimum risk to the mission and maximum risk to them.

He told Nanos and Billy Two to hit the bottom of the door on the count of three. On the count of two, Barrabas stepped out of the dead space into the middle of the lane of fire and put a short burst through the lock. O'Toole and Hayes moved to his right and left, angled to take out Pasdars on the sides.

On three, Nanos and Billy Two hit the door in unison. The barricade of crates screeched and toppled as the door swung inward. Even as the door began to move, a terrible cry rose up from the rad lab. Leaderless, perhaps mindless as well, the trapped Pasdars charged the opening door. They were so frantic to kill, to avenge the deaths of comrades, to defend the honor of their precious bunker that even though they fired as they ran, they jostled for position, bumping shoulders, knocking off each other's aim.

Slugs whipped past Barrabas's head, whacking into the sandbags behind him. They registered as shadows in the back of his mind. Distant, unrelated to the frantic compression of time, space and fury before him. Barrabas looked straight into the face of onrushing death, his teeth bared, his index finger pinning back the XM-177's trigger. His weapon played music.

Rock and roll music.

The human wave of zealots met an inhuman wave of bullets. The first five went down. Then five more. The final pair of Pasdars died as they tried to jump the crates.

The SOBs surged into the rad lab, turning over the dead, checking the room for hiding places. When Barrabas was sure they had control, he turned to Beck and said, "Time to do your stuff."

The electronics genius looked over the room's contents for a few seconds before he turned back to the colonel. "We've got big problems," he said.

"We can't detonate?"

"Oh, sure, we can detonate, all right. But we're missing one goddamn bomb."

"It's got to be here," Barrabas said. "Go ahead, Nate, rig one of them to blow. Nanos, Claude, you two come with me. We'll check the other rooms along the hall."

A search of the metal shop and electronics lab turned up nothing.

"It could be in there with the last of the Pasdars," Nanos said, pointing at the explosives storage room.

"Yeah, it could," Barrabas agreed. As he surveyed the heavy metal door a scowl spread over his face. "But we're never going to get through all that steel to find out."

There were other possibilities as well. Jessup could have gotten some bum data from his sneaky petes. Maybe there never was a fourth bomb. Or maybe it was still in component form stored somewhere above ground.

All those alternatives were acceptable.

Unacceptable was the chance that the fourth bomb had already been removed from the site and was on the way to its target.

Another man might have looked for a bright side to the situation and been satisfied with the confirmed destruction of three-fourths of the Iranian atomic arsenal; for Nile Barrabas there was no bright side to the potential loss of a hundred thousand innocent lives.

His options were slim and none. He had to play it as if they had containment. Destroy the three weapons and get his people the hell out.

When they returned to the rad lab, Beck was poring over sheaves of wiring diagrams. He looked up and said, "Did you find it?"

Barrabas shook his head. "How's it going?"

"Well, it could be a hell of a lot worse. This beauty is fitted out with several different kinds of antitampering devices. Only they don't engage until the bomb's detonation timer is activated. Otherwise, it could go off if it was accidentally mishandled in transit."

"Not much point in booby trapping something if there's a chance you're going to be the one to set it off," Nanos said.

"You got it."

"How much longer?" Barrabas asked.

"It looks like maybe ten minutes. I've got to cut out their timer and splice in ours."

"Take your time," Barrabas told him. "Do it right."

17

"Jesus, what's taking them so long?" Biondi said as he looked out the window of the Sikorsky. The view from the copilot's seat was perfect. The camp below was tiny, a fairy ring of lights; inside the ring, scattered fires flickered.

"It hasn't been all that long," Gunther told him. "They're still well within the time limit. We've got nothing to worry about, yet."

"We could buzz a little lower and make sure."

Gunther frowned. "The colonel said for us to stay at five thousand feet until he gives us the signal for the pickup."

"I feel so goddamn useless up here."

"Join the club."

"So, let's *do* something about it."

"Hey, man, Barrabas knows best. We just follow orders and let him worry about whether or not our talents are being wasted."

"Yeah, you're right."

As Gunther banked the helicopter he glanced over at Biondi. He got the unsettling feeling that his copilot could have flown on without mechanical assistance, on sheer suppressed rage. The episode with the Iranian colonel was still tender in Gunther's memory. And he was damned glad that Biondi was not on the ground with an automatic weapon in his hands.

The Dutchman had dealt with a lot of loony tunes the world over. He had found a general type that crossed all national, racial and religious borders. The hair-trigger type. Like Biondi. A hell of a guy to have at your back in an all-out firefight. A danger in situations when something less was in order. It was as if the guy only knew one way to live: full bore.

All the SOBs were like that, to varying degrees. Gunther, a man circling a mile over ground zero, could not exactly claim to be normal himself. But if the other SOBs were sky-rockets in flight, Vince Biondi was a goddamn comet.

"Hey!" Gunther said, pointing out his side window. "What the hell are those?"

"What? Where? I don't see anything."

"They disappeared. A string of lights. Off to the east at eleven o'clock. Look! There they are again!"

"HOW MUCH TIME do you want before detonation?" Beck asked Barrabas.

"Five minutes to get out. Fifteen more to put some miles between us and here."

Beck punched the numbers into the timer. "Say when." His thumb hovered over the start button.

"If that bomb blows when you push that thing," Nanos said, "I'm never going to forgive you."

"Is everybody ready?" Barrabas said. "Where's Hayes?"

"He went back down the hallway a minute ago," O'Toole said.

"Punch the button and let's get him."

Beck activated the timer, and the SOBs hurried from the rad lab.

As they reached the main hallway a godawful bellowing erupted from the direction of the explosives room. Then Hayes appeared, also from that direction.

"What the hell is going on back there?" O'Toole asked.

Hayes shrugged as he joined them. "I speak a little bit of Pharsee."

"Yeah?"

"So, I thought those guys we locked in should know what's about to happen to them. So they can get their lives in order. Say their last prayers, whatever."

The bellowing had quickly risen in pitch until it was one long unbroken scream.

"You owed them that much," Nanos said.

"Yeah, that's what I thought, too."

The air outside the bunker was fresh and clean. A slight breeze had sprung up, blowing away the smell of burned meat.

O'Toole dug a flare pistol from his pack and fired off a shot. Green for go. While they were waiting for the pickup, Barrabas and Hayes found an operational jeep. They got it started, then drove it down the bunker's ramp. They left its front end jammed against the steel doors.

The Sikorsky was just touching down outside the camp gates when they finished. By the time they gathered up their gear and radioed the copter, the other SOBs were aboard.

Barrabas was the last to step in. The bad news about Chen and Boone and the fourth weapon had already been passed on.

"I should've been there," Biondi said. "I should've."

The swoosh of the rotors blotted out his voice.

As Gunther lifted the chopper off, he yelled back at Barrabas, "We saw some lights on the road to the east while we were circling. Could be our missing bomb."

"How far away?"

"Five miles, maybe."

Barrabas checked his watch. "I make it sixteen-oh-five until detonation."

"Right," Beck said.

"We've got time for a looksee."

"Whew!" Nanos said, shuddering.

"What's wrong?" Billy Two asked him.

"The short hairs, man. The short hairs."

They all knew exactly what the Greek meant.

18

For the third time in less than a mile, Captain Razod made his driver honk the truck's horn, bringing the convoy to a halt.

He got out of the passenger door and listened carefully, straining to hear.

Yes, there it was again. Sporadic gunfire. And a deeper sound. Like rolling thunder. He looked into the cloudless sky. It was manmade thunder.

A chill rippled his backbone.

The camp was under attack, of that he had no doubt. How it had come about and who was staging it he could only guess: the Iraqi swine? The stooges of imperialist Amrika? The Zionist gangsters? He was confident that no matter how concerted the assault, his men would be able to retreat to the bunker and call for aid from Kerman. Call for an air strike to annihilate the enemy.

That did not solve his current problem. In fact, it added to it. If the attackers were driven back or grew tired of trying to open the bunker, they might seek other targets.

Easy targets.

The Pasdars looked worried. They had a perfect right to be. Out on the open road, they were sitting ducks.

"Back in the trucks!" Razod shouted at the drivers. "Move! Move!"

He climbed in himself, cursing the darkness. They had to run with headlights on or risk driving off the road. As the convoy lumbered forward, Razod unfolded a map and with the aid of a penlight tried to find someplace ahead large enough to conceal three trucks and a jeep.

It was hopeless.

There was not so much as a tree for miles. No side roads. No tunnels. Only the dirt track winding up, down and between the hills.

As he crushed the map in his fist, the penlight swept over the pious visage pasted to the dash. Those gleaming zealot's eyes spoke to Razod, entreating him to use his native cunning, to find a way to save the precious cargo from capture or destruction.

"Aha!" Razod said, slapping the seat.

It was so easy after all.

The attacking force would have its sitting ducks and be satisfied. But Mohamadi Razod would not be among them. He would wait until they got to the bottom of the grade they were now on, then find a nice hard place for the driver to pull off. He would let the other trucks continue on, their headlights blazing, while he sat in the shadows of some lonely hill waiting for dawn to break and help to arrive.

"Jackpot!" Gunther exclaimed.

"Where?" Barrabas said.

"Right there," Biondi told him, pointing out the string of headlights on the road before them. They disappeared one by one as the convoy went around a turn.

"I count three trucks and a jeep leading," Gunther said.

"It's got to be our baby," Barrabas said. He turned back to the SOBs. "Load up three Bloopers with HE and get the left door open. Don't hit any of the trucks. Take out the jeep and as much of the roadway as you can. I don't want them moving past the line we draw in the dirt."

O'Toole, Nanos and Billy Two plugged the breeches of their grenade launchers with 40mm projectiles. The other mercs dumped half-empty mags for full ones.

"How much time left, Nate?"

"Fourteen minutes."

"Holy shit," Nanos groaned.

"Shut up, Alex," Billy Two said. "You know you're lovin' every second of it."

"After we hit the road, Gunther," Barrabas said, "I want you to swing around and drop us behind them. Everybody listen up. We've got to hit and git. Don't spare the ammo. All right, Gunther, take us in.''

O'Toole, Nanos and Billy Two sat braced by the open door, the sling straps of their M-79s wrapped around forearms. Gunther brought the Sikorsky in low and slow from behind, matching the convoy's speed.

"Do it!" Barrabas said.

The three guns spoke. No sooner were the projectiles away than the SOBs were cracking open the breeches of their grenade launchers. They were shoving fresh rounds home when the HE triple-punch landed.

Blossoms of orange billowing fire lit up the road below. The bass rumble of the explosions came up to them a second late. The lead jeep did not take a direct hit, but it rolled right through one of the blasts. Its driver and passengers toppled out onto the road. Its hood belching flames, the jeep bounded off the track and crashed to a stop against a boulder.

The closely following trucks slammed on their brakes to avoid the second volley of grenades from the Sikorsky, a volley that gnawed up great hunks of the roadway.

Gunther crossed the road and swung back, heading for the new LZ.

RAZOD HEARD THE SIKORSKY before he saw it, a vicious droning sound sweeping up on them from behind.

He stuck his head out the window, and there it was.

Black against the stars.

"No!" he cried as he helplessly watched the helicopter slide ahead. It looked close enough to touch. The Pasdars in the truck in front were not firing. "Honk! Honk, damn you!" he shouted at his driver.

Too late.

Blue flame winked from the center of the sliding shadow.

As the driver hit his horn, the grenades hit the road. Razod saw the bright flashes of light, heard the trio of solid whumps, then the truck in front of them began to swerve crazily back and forth.

His driver swerved, too, when he saw the size of the smoldering craters dead ahead. He caught the edge of one with his right front wheel. Razod's head bumped into the cab's ceiling as the truck dropped down, then bounced up and out of the hole.

Out his side window Razod could see the jeep running off the road into a field of boulders.

Everything was coming apart. He clung to the door handle with both hands when the second barrage landed.

The truck in front came to a screeching, skidding stop.

Razod's driver cut to the left of the halted vehicle and hit his own brakes. The truck behind it swung to the right.

The captain had his door open before the vehicle came to a full stop. "Back it up!" he told the driver as he jumped down. "Turn it around!"

He dashed to the nearest troop truck and slammed his hand against its wooden side. "Out! Out!" he shouted at the Pasdars who were still trying to untangle themselves after the sudden stop.

The Sikorsky had turned and was heading back in the direction it had come.

"Quick! Shoot! Shoot!" he cried.

The guardsmen were too slow in forming up.

The helicopter was getting smaller, its outline less distinct against the stars. Razod drew his side arm. Taking a one-handed dueling stance, he opened up with the Beretta. He got off three shots before the craft disappeared behind the back of a hill.

The truck with the bomb backed up and turned, spinning its tires. It banged its rear end into a fender of one of the other vehicles. The driver was grinding gears, fighting with the steering wheel.

"Sergeant," Razod said, "get your men in position along the edge of the road. Under the trucks. The weapon must be defended to the death. Do you understand?"

The noncom nodded and began to deploy the Pasdars around the stopped trucks.

"Cut the lights!" Razod ordered the drivers.

The roadway was plunged into darkness. It took several seconds for Razod's eyes to adjust. When he could see again, he moved quickly between the troop trucks and positioned himself in the most secure spot he could find, the deep shadow behind the tailgate of the bomb truck.

Whoever the attackers were, they would have hell to pay if they tried to take the weapon, Razod thought. Darkness was now the Pasdars' ally.

GUNTHER TOUCHED THE SIKORSKY DOWN on the dirt road a quarter mile uphill from the convoy. Barrabas did not have to tell the SOBs to get the lead out. They hit the road running.

"Give us a minute," he told Gunther and Biondi.

Then he ran down the road, too.

The others were waiting just around a bend. They crept around it and looked down a slightly steeper grade to the flat stretch where the convoy was stopped. It was too dark to make out much more than the overall shapes of the trucks. It was a safe bet that the Pasdars could not see them at all.

Barrabas gestured for the rest of the sniper team to fan out across the road. They quickly set up the four M-21s.

Barrabas bellied down behind the rifle, turned on the scope and put his eye to the lens. He picked out targets in the ditch alongside the road and under the trucks. In the back of his mind he could hear clicks as the numbers fell. Come on, Gunther, he thought. Now's the time.

The Sikorsky roared around the hill and swooped over them at about one hundred fifty feet. It dived at the stationary trucks, then veered off to the right.

With shouts of righteous fury, the Pasdars scrambled out from under the trucks, jumped up from the ditches to pour small-arms fire at the fast-disappearing helicopter.

Barrabas held the cross hairs on the middle of a back and squeezed the trigger. The silenced weapon barely coughed. He swung the sights onto a head and tightened down. Again the weak cough, the plink of a spent cartridge in the dirt.

Beside him, O'Toole, Billy Two and Hayes were working the same kind of dark magic: searching for a man-shape amid the yellow-green field, pinning it in the cross hairs, then pinning it with lead.

Four long guns working in concert cut into the Pasdar numbers in a hurry. After a minute it was hard to find a standing target.

Barrabas lined up on one man only to see him fold before he could pull the trigger.

Somebody down in the convoy yelled something, and the remaining guardsmen dived for cover.

They had finally wised up. But not before the SOBs had reduced the odds.

IT PAINED HIM to admit it to himself, but Captain Razod had been fooled, too.

He had been one of the first to jump out from cover and fire at the retreating shape of the helicopter. He had even called for his men to follow his example. In the rage of gunfire that ensued it was impossible to hear the enemy bullets whining among them. In the pitch darkness it was difficult to see the men fall.

Razod had come to an immediate understanding of the situation only after the back of his neck was splashed with blood. He turned in time to see the man behind him drop. It was then that he shouted the alarm.

From beneath the bed of the bomb truck he could see the road littered with bodies. He had lost half his men without even seeing the enemy.

A man to his left groaned.

Had Razod heard the whistle of a bullet an instant before? The thud of impact? He could not be sure. The sound of his own blood pounding in his ears, the rasp of his breathing, all but deafened him.

The captain reached out a foot and kicked the man. The torso moved without resisting, like it was made of gelatin. However the enemy was killing in the dark, one thing was perfectly clear to Razod: he was no longer safe where he was.

Leaving his empty Beretta in the dirt, he clambered up onto the bomb truck's rear bumper, then over the tailgate and onto the bed. On hands and knees he crawled over to the big wooden crate. Between it and the cab of the truck was a very small space. As Razod squeezed into it, he looked through the little window in the back of the cab. Starlight reflected crazily off the truck's front windshield, a spiderweb of silver, in the center of which was a crusty round hole.

The driver was on his side on the seat. He was not moving. He had died with the engine running.

Razod slipped down into the space.

BARRABAS SWEPT the view field of the nightscope from one side of the road, under the facing truck, to the other. There were no more targets. All the surviving Pasdars had moved back under cover of the pair of trucks headed the other way.

It was time to flush them out.

He traded his M-21 for an M-79 and loaded it with a CS gas shell. O'Toole fired the flare gun, aiming it directly over the convoy. The green light came on, trailing pale green smoke that drifted from right to left.

That was all Barrabas, Beck and Hayes needed to know. The three of them laid down a barrage of teargas on the right side of the trucks. White cottony smoke erupted from the ruptured shells, flowing smoothly under the wheels and out the other side.

Before the flare went out, they put down another trio of gas shells, dropping them even closer to the pair of trucks. A river of CS rushed under them. As the green light faded, dark figures crawled, then stumbled away from the underside of the downwind truck, stumbled over the boulder-littered field in the midst of a swirling white cloud.

And as they did, they once again became targets.

On the road in front of Barrabas the quartet of M-21s began to talk. And off in the pitch darkness, men fell, their death agonies witnessed only by those who killed them.

When the sniper fire stopped, Barrabas used a spotting scope to survey the convoy. Nothing moved. Still, they would make sure before calling down the Sikorsky.

The SOBs quickly, quietly filtered down the road. The teargas was spent, blown away by a steady breeze. They checked under the trucks, looked inside them, then Barrabas signaled for Gunther to return. A red flare.

The helicopter dropped down, then hovered at one hundred feet. Its powerful searchlight blinked on, illuminating the war zone in hard white light.

Beck gestured at the back of one of the trucks. He and Barrabas looked over the tailgate. The

light through the rear entrance of the truck's canvas cover was bright enough to see the big
wooden crate.

"We sure got lucky," Beck said.

"Did we? How much time do we have left?"

"Eight minutes."

"That's not enough. Get Gunther down on the
double."

19

Mohamadi Razod jerked violently when the flare burst overhead, flooding the truck bed with eerie green light. He steeled himself for the worst, an all-out attack by a superior ground force or a barrage of air-to-ground missiles.

In either case, he had picked the wrong place to hide. And with the whole area bathed in light, it was too late to run.

He flinched again when the first of the teargas shells exploded behind him. It was a soft popping sound, not the brittle crack of something truly dangerous.

Then he smelled it.

He knew what it was at once. It raged up his nose and peppered his eyes. By no means did he get the dose of CS that the men under the other trucks got. He was on the fringe of the gas flow. He cried, he gagged, but it was not enough to drive him from his hiding place. Even the second volley did not budge him.

The green light dwindled, then vanished.

Outside, over the low rumble of the idling truck engine, he could hear the coughs and moans of the Pasdars as they were forced from places of safety. Every once in a while their anguished cries were punctuated by a sharp thwack. He knew that sound. Guardsmen were dying out there, being shot from a distance.

After a couple of minutes the moaning and the kill sounds stopped. He tried to burrow down into the bed of the truck. He prayed that somehow he would be spared. He offered to perform great, selfless deeds for his country, if only the miracle would come to pass.

Footsteps, light and quick, moved around the truck.

Razod held his breath.

Someone was opening the tailgate, drawing back the rusty bolts that held it closed.

Make me invisible, he thought. Make them blind.

The truck bed shifted as someone climbed up into it, but there was no cry of discovery, no bullet to the neck. The truck shuddered again as whoever it was departed. God had answered him.

After a little while he began to hear voices close by. Then the sound of a helicopter dropping down directly over him. When the searchlight came on he almost screamed. It was so bright in the bed of the truck that he could see the wood of the crate next to his nose.

Again there were voices, louder and closer. He could not understand the words, but he knew what the language was: English. The tongue of the Great Satan himself. And at once he had many answers. He knew who had attacked the camp and the convoy, and he knew why. Amrika wanted to take back its idol.

Razod was no longer afraid. Clearly God had spared him for some monumental task and would continue to shield him from harm until that task was completed.

The voices from the rear of the truck faded away. The light of the helicopter switched off, and the machine moved to the side and landed.

The captain relaxed in the narrow space, content to wait for the hand of God to show him the way.

BARRABAS GATHERED all the mercs together in front of the bomb truck, far enough away from the rotorwash of the idling Sikorsky so he could be heard. What he had to say hacked at his heart.

"Right now we have a little more than seven minutes until detonation. That's not enough time to return the fourth weapon to the camp and get away, even if we already had it secured to the Sikorsky."

"How far away could we get?" Beck asked.

"Five or six miles at most," Gunther answered.

"The shock front would probably knock the helicopter out of the air," Barrabas said. "And even if it didn't, we'd all be badly, maybe critically burned.''

"So, what are you saying?" Biondi demanded.

"We're in a no-win. If we leave the bomb where it is, the Iranians will use it on somebody."

"Then let's wreck it," Billy Two said.

"How? With what?" Barrabas asked. "You saw what those cases look like. Nothing we've got would even dent one. And besides, there's still the time factor."

"So it was all for nothing," Nanos said.

He did not have to say Chen and Boone. It was what they all were thinking.

"To hell with that!" O'Toole snarled. "Let's load the sucker up and take our chances."

It was what Barrabas wanted to do.

What he could not order.

He had to give his soldiers a chance to bail out.

The SOBs did not want a way out.

They all agreed with O'Toole.

All except Vince Biondi. He had another solution to the fix they were in. One that would cost only a single life.

His.

While the others were hurrying to get the helicopter ready, Biondi opened the door of the bomb truck, dumped the dead driver out then slipped behind the wheel. He gave the engine a goose, rammed it into gear and popped the clutch.

The truck lurched forward.

Barrabas and O'Toole had to jump out of the way or be run over.

"Biondi, you crazy jerk, get out of there!" Barrabas yelled at him, breaking into a full sprint to keep pace with the accelerating vehicle.

O'Toole was running right by his side. "Vince! Jesus, Vince!"

Biondi shifted into second, boring up the grade. As he did so, he stuck his head out the open window and said, "See you guys you-know-where."

Then he pulled away. The cloud of dust he raised obscured the view in the side mirror. He should not have been looking back anyway, he told himself. He turned on the truck's high beams. Never look back. Never.

Biondi did not consider what he was doing in any way heroic. To him it was just flat-out logic. There was only one way to get the bomb back to the camp inside of six minutes with minimum loss of personnel and that was to goddamn drive it there. Of all the SOBs, he was the only one with the skill to beat the clock.

As the truck reached the top of the grade, Biondi jammed it into third and flattened the gas pedal to the floorboards.

"Come on, you old bitch," he yelled. "This is the last roundup for both of us."

Then he laughed.

"Do you know I've spent most of my adult life trying to kill myself in something with wheels? Oh yeah, it was always called a race. With big bucks and glory waiting at the finish line. Hey, for me it was an excuse to get out there and put it all on the line. I never gave a damn about winning."

He laughed again.

"Now, not only am I in a race that I lose if I win," he said, "but I'm going to eat the Big One in some patched-together rolling shit heap. When I think of all the fine precision-crafted machines I've totaled and walked away from, this has got to be some kind of justice."

The ruts in the road made the wheel jump and jitter between his hands. He bounced on the seat but kept the truck under control, squeezing every bit of downhill speed out of it.

He hit the bottom of the grade and started back up, waiting until the perfect moment to shift. The lever slipped into place without so much as a chirp. The engine, on the other hand, bellowed under the sudden added load.

"Come on, baby. You can take it," he said as they chugged up the slope. "You can take it all."

The truck could take it, all right, but slowly. Infuriatingly slowly.

Biondi glanced at the dash and for the first time saw the picture pasted there.

"Well, well, what have we here?" he said. "I

had some company along and didn't even know it. And, hey, do you know, I can't think of anyone else I'd rather be making this trip with. You and me, sweetheart, straight into the dripping jaws of you-know-what. Shit, if the gas wasn't already on you, I'd pick up the tab.''

MOHAMADI RAZOD stayed behind the crate for as long as he dared. Whoever was driving the truck was going so fast and weaving so wildly that he was making the heavy crate shift. Razod was afraid of being crushed to death by it.

When he slipped out, he carefully peeked into the cab's rear window. It was difficult to keep on his feet, the way the truck was bouncing and shaking. There was a little light from the instrument panel. In the glow he could see the driver. A swarthy skinned man with black hair. He could have been a Pasdar except that he was speaking English, shouting it at the top of his lungs.

Razod was being driven away by a madman.

He had to be mad. He was heading back for the Pasdar camp. Taking the nuclear device back where it belonged.

When they had roared away from the ambush site, Razod had heard the other men yelling at the driver. Whatever he was doing, it was not part of Satan's plan.

It was logical, then, he told himself, that the

plan was God's own. That the driver had been possessed and forced to do God's will.

It was enough that the man had rescued him from the hands of his enemies. If Razod had not left his pistol behind, he would have used it, through the window, to stop the driver and the maniacal pace he was setting for the ancient truck.

As it was, Razod had no weapon to use against the man. And the closer they came to the camp, the more he began to worry that the perimeter guards might not understand the situation. After all, they had just undergone an attack by foreign criminals. What if the driver tried to crash the gates? What if they did not recognize the truck?

The captain had come to the conclusion that he had to jump from the moving vehicle and walk the rest of the way back to the camp. The only problem was that the truck was going too fast for him to jump with any degree of safety.

He would have to wait for an uphill grade, then take his chances.

While he waited, he watched the driver and listened to his unintelligible raving. It became clear after a moment or two that the man was speaking to the picture stuck to the dash. Whatever he was saying or doing, there seemed to be a kind of pattern. He would rant for a few sentences, then make a hand gesture.

It was, perhaps, a kind of a salute. If so, Razod had never seen it before. The fist clenched and the middle finger upraised.

Then the truck hit a long steep grade.

Razod crawled to the tailgate, slipped a leg over and was readying himself to jump when the rear wheels hit a bump. He was pitched clear of the truck bed and landed on his side in the middle of the road. He slightly twisted his ankle in the fall.

He struggled to his feet and tried to take his bearings from the surroundings. It was a good thing he had only three miles to walk back to camp because his ankle was very sore.

BIONDI WAS ON THE HOMESTRETCH. He could not see the camp yet, but it would not be long. Ahead of him were a series of switchbacks, all leading down to the plain, to the mile and a half of straight road that led to the camp gates.

"I wonder if I'm going to feel anything?" he said. "If it's going to hurt?"

He scowled at the picture on the dash.

"Come on, Swami, lay it on me. What's the Biondi boy's future look like? A long and happy life? Six squealers and a pair of Labs? Or is old Vince just going to be another flash in the pan?"

The road ahead was beginning to straighten out. And the skyline was brightened by the camp's floodlights in the near distance.

"Do you know why I hate your guts, Swami? It isn't because you're different. Lots of people are weird. Hell, I'm weird. It's because you're one genuine, Grade A raging asshole. So, maybe it's not all your fault. Maybe there's something about this dump, something in the air or the dirt that just breeds assholes. That would sure explain your share of the world market."

As the ravaged camp complex came into view, Biondi's hands tightened on the wheel. "Yeah! We're gonna make it. Make it all the way!"

He had a sudden worrisome thought. "Wouldn't it be swell if Nate set the fucking timer wrong? And after breaking my balls to get this junk pile to ground zero in six minutes, I had to wait around for half an hour to get vaporized? Yeah, that would sure take some of the zing out of it for me."

Biondi roared down the straightaway at absolute maximum speed. He was no longer steering the beast. It was a runaway freight. He and the Swami were along for the ride.

"Come on! Come on!" he cried, bouncing up and down on the seat, trying to coax a little more speed out of the wreck.

The camp's shattered gates rushed up at him very fast. Before he could blink he was crashing through the compound, heading straight for the bunker ramp.

"God, I hope this is quick," he said. Then he shouted at the picture on the dash, "And as for you, Jack, *va fan . . . .*"

It was quick.

20

Captain Razod stopped to rest his sore foot. He sat down on a large boulder and removed his boot. His ankle was badly swollen and it hurt when he tried to curl his toes. He wondered if he had broken something. He had only covered twenty yards since his last rest stop. At the rate he was going, it would take him the remainder of the night to reach camp. Perhaps that was not the best idea, after all. He could wait by the side of the road until a vehicle passed. After the attack there would certainly be some movement, either to or from the compound.

It was cold. He tried to keep his mind off of his various discomforts by imagining what greater glory God had saved him for.

A place on the Revolutionary Council? He hoped not. Better a judgeship. Yes, that was something he knew he would enjoy.

His eyes were slipping shut when it happened.

A light behind him.

Pure blue light so powerful against his back that it cast his shadow a hundred feet in front of him. He started to turn and look into the brightness, but paused.

Something was terribly wrong.

A booming wall of wind slammed him, knocking him into the air like a leaf. He tumbled amid lighter bits of debris, then crashed to the rocks and rolled. Rolled until a boulder stopped him. He lay pinned facedown while some monstrous thing pressed his back. He felt his ribs snapping like dry twigs. He tried to scream against the battering gale but there was no air in his lungs, only blood.

Blackness swarmed over him like a vast, frantic army of ants.

"Now," NATE BECK SAID, looking up from his watch.

As if by his command, it dawned.

It dawned two hours early over south-central Iran.

It was a false dawn that lasted only a second.

It gave no warmth, no comfort to anyone. Least of all to the Soldiers of Barrabas. They were speeding away, high and safe, from a place of much death. A charnel house. An inferno. Leaving friends behind.

THE WORLD WAS ON FIRE when Mohamadi Razod regained consciousness.

No, that was not true.

Over his head, tiny points of light glittered against a field of black. It was still night. It was Razod who was on fire. It was inside him, inside his skull, turning the walls bright, bright blue.

He screamed, and a terrible broken animal sound burst from his throat. He burned. From head to foot he was encased in flame.

He raised his hands to heaven and felt a heavy, dragging weight.

His clothes hung in tatters.

No, he had no clothes. He was naked. What hung down from his arms and chest was skin.

Again he cried out.

He had a savage thirst. His own tongue was choking him, gagging him.

He tried to rise and collapsed. There was something wrong with his left leg, something poking out of it at a right angle. It was a stick, a bloody stick. He pulled on it. It was bone.

His bone.

Despite the broken limb, he tried to force himself up. There was a seething restlessness within him that was even stronger than the pain. He did not recognize the horrible, fluttering unease for what it was, his spirit's refusal to give in to the inevitable, to give up its hold on the ruined flesh.

All Razod knew was that he had to move, to walk.

Where, it did not matter.

He staggered off across the sea of stones, trailing his own skin like a shroud. His reward for services rendered lay ahead, somewhere in the darkness and desolation.

This was what his God had saved him for.

21

Barrabas sat in the back corner of a gritty Amsterdam coffeehouse, staring at the front page of the *International Herald-Tribune*. The cigar trapped between his teeth had long since gone out, the tiny cup of triple-strength coffee at his elbow was cold.

The banner headline before him said Iran Still Denies A-Blast. He read the article.

TEHRAN, Iran (Reuters)—Iranian government officials continue heated denials that an atomic detonation took place within its borders early last Wednesday morning. This despite new evidence from the international scientific community.

Seismic recordings gathered from worldwide monitoring stations and correlated by the Hagfors Observatory, Sweden, indicate that an atomic explosion of between 30 and 50 kilotons occurred in south-central Iran at 2:36 A.M. on the 20th of July. The epicenter of the blast was estimated to be 125 miles southeast of Kerman.

This confirms data presented earlier by the United States Department of Defense taken from its Early Warning Satellites.

Atmospheric radioactive samplings conducted independently by both the French and the Israelis have also verified the U.S. contention that this was one of the dirtiest bombs ever exploded.

Iran's refusal to acknowledge the blast has further fueled speculation among the world's scientists that it was unintentional, an accident of unparalleled magnitude.

In response to today's disclosures, Pakistan has called for a special session of the United Nations Security Council. Elsewhere around the world, condemnation of the apparent weapons test has been almost unanimous.

High State Department sources predict some sort of unified international economic censure will be brought against Iran within the next two weeks.

Barrabas read the story over and over. There was no hint that an outside force was involved. There never would be.

Mission accomplished.

Cash in the bank.

Barrabas chewed his cigar. He did not like how he felt. He knew it would pass, and he liked that even less.

He was a mercenary. A guy who fought for money. That was the definition, all right. Only there was more to it than the dictionary let on. Much more. Sure, mercs fought for pay, but they did not die for it.

They died for comrades.

They died for total strangers.

He kept thinking about three men who had given their all, knowing they would never get credit for the sacrifice.

No newspaper headlines.

No national day of mourning.

No made-for-TV movies.

Barrabas looked at the photograph below the screaming headline again. It was a high-altitude recon shot. Three good guys had died unnoticed by the world, as if they had simply disappeared, but their passing had left its mark.

At the edge of a plain in a land of rocks there was a hole a half mile across. It would be there long after the country that surrounded it was forgotten.

Barrabas clenched the cigar between his teeth.

Chen.

Boone.

Biondi.

Yeah, their monument would last ten thousand years.

JACK HILD

The editors at Gold Eagle asked Jack Hild to fill this space with a short autobiographical sketch.

He responded by sending us three telephone numbers.

One belonged to an ex-wife, his fourth or fifth; she wasn't sure. One belonged to a partner in a now-defunct import-export business specializing in "farm machinery." And the last turned out to be the Los Angeles office of the Internal Revenue Service, Criminal Investigation Division.

All three were very much interested in Mr. Hild's current whereabouts.

Information that we were unable to supply.

What readers are saying about The SOBs

"As a member of the UN peacekeeping force in the Congo and other spots, not to mention action in Korea and Indochina, I have to say your research is damn accurate!"
—*M.B., Bedford, PQ*

"The Soldiers of Barrabas care, but they have to hide the fact behind a to-hell-with-it attitude so necessary in their situation. Very well written, a winner in all respects. There's a great future for this group!"
—*P.R., Calgary, Alberta*

"My favorite character is Nile Barrabas. It's not often a reader gets this kind of a thrill."
—*J.B., Tishomingo, OK*

"I'm in love with Leona Hatton. She's intelligent, independent, not afraid of being a woman. The SOBs show that small unit tactics can work really well when professionally applied."
—*S.R., Springfield, MA*

"What a great bunch of guys."
—*S.B., Bellflower, CA*

"The SOBs will do all right!"
—*D.H., Willowick, OH*

GOLD EAGLE